"Look, Jade, I know that after all that's happened between us I'm asking a lot...

"But don't you see? If I introduce you as my wife it will seriously undermine the Turners' case, and with any luck the judge will throw out this new application of theirs to try to gain custody of Matthew."

"But are you sure it will work?" Jade asked, and felt her heart flutter when Evan brought his hands up to grasp her shoulders.

"Right now I'm not sure of anything," he told her in a heavy voice. "All I know is I have to do something. Will you help me?"

Beneath his hands a familiar heat began to radiate through her, arousing forgotten sensations, forbidden needs.

"Yes, I'll marry you," Jade said.

Moyra Tarling is the youngest of four children born and raised in Aberdeenshire, Scotland. It was there that she was first introduced to and became hooked on romance novels. After emigrating to Vancouver, Canada, Ms Tarling met her future husband, Noel, at a party in Birch Bay—and promptly fell in love. They now have two children. Together they enjoy browsing through antiques shops and auctions, looking for various items, from old gramophones to antique corkscrews and buttonhooks.

MARRY IN HASTE

BY
MOYRA TARLING

For my aunt Peggy who, in her ninety-seventh year,
is still young at heart. Much love.

*First published in Great Britain 2000
Harlequin Mills & Boon Limited,
Eton House, 18-24 Paradise Road, Richmond, Surrey TW9 1SR*

© Moyra Tarling 1997

ISBN 0 263 82026 2

*Set in Times Roman 10½ on 12 pt.
01-0010-44482*

*Printed and bound in Spain
by Litografia Rosés, S.A., Barcelona*

Chapter One

"Hank! Hank! Are you there?" Jade Adams called out anxiously as she let herself into her god-father's cabin on Paradise Lake.

As the cabin door closed behind her, Jade held her breath listening for a response. But the only sound she could hear was the winter storm howling outside.

Concern and fear for Hank Mathieson's, well-being had her hurrying down the hall to the living room, brushing snowflakes from her hair as she went. She'd been trying to contact Hank for the past three days, to no avail. She'd even called several of his friends in nearby Paradise to ask if they'd seen or heard from him. No one had.

That's why she'd spent the last two and a half hours driving through an Oregon snowfall in a car not properly equipped for the winter weather.

The expansive living room was almost in total

darkness, the heavy drapes drawn across the big bay window shutting out the chilly November night. A lamp standing in the far corner was the only source of light, giving off a muted and eerie glow.

A shiver chased down Jade's spine as she scanned the room in search of her godfather.

Suddenly something caught her eye, bringing her attention to the big old chair near the fireplace.

"Hank? Is that you? Are you all right?" Her questions were met with silence and Jade's heart leapt into her throat. Had her worst fear indeed come to pass?

All at once the old recliner creaked in protest as a shadowy figure moved. "Hank's not here." The deep rich voice was instantly recognizable and brought a startled gasp to Jade's lips.

"Evan?" The name came out in a breathless whisper. She had to be dreaming! Evan couldn't be here. The last she'd heard he still worked as a news correspondent for a television news station in Boston.

It was a job he loved, a job that entailed a great deal of traveling, a job Evan found infinitely challenging but one that Jade, during their brief engagement, had grown to hate.

During the four months they'd been engaged she'd accompanied him on several of his assignments, soon realizing there was nothing remotely romantic or idyllic about living out of a suitcase or sitting in a hotel room for hours waiting for him to return.

"It's me, in the flesh," Evan drawled as he slowly unwound his six-foot frame from the depths of his father's rocker-recliner. Dressed in a pair of brown cord pants and tan-colored shirt, he looked decidedly arresting and achingly familiar.

A shudder tore through Jade and she hugged herself, trying to stop her body from trembling, glad of the shadowy darkness that helped hide her reaction. Unprepared as she was to find Evan there, she was determined not to let him see she was affected in any way by his presence.

"Wha...what are you doing here?" she asked, annoyed that her voice wavered slightly.

"More to the point, what are *you* doing here?" Evan countered, taking a step toward her, his piercing blue eyes meeting hers in a look that held a mixture of arrogance and challenge.

Tempted as she was to retreat, Jade refused to feel intimidated. Bravely she held his gaze. "I came to check on your father," she said. "I've been trying to get through to him on the telephone for days but there was no answer."

"Concerned about him, were you?" Evan asked, his tone silky and deceptively smooth.

"Of course I was," Jade replied, not bothering to hide her annoyance.

"And so you drove through a snowstorm just to find out if he was all right," Evan went on as he crossed to an end table nearby to switch on a lamp.

Jade blinked at the sudden brightness, which brought Evan's strikingly handsome features into sharp focus. "Yes," she responded, ignoring the familiar leap of her pulse.

"I'm impressed," Evan commented dryly.

Jade flinched inwardly as his comment found its

mark. She heard the reproach in his voice and knew he expected her to retaliate. But she refused to give him the satisfaction and clamped down on the impulse to defend herself.

"I came to check on Hank, not to argue with you," she said with as much cool as she could muster, and caught the look of surprise that flickered in Evan's striking blue eyes before he turned and crossed to the liquor cabinet standing against the wall.

Evan had been referring, of course, to the fact that she hadn't returned to New Orleans to be by his side after the tragic deaths of his best friends, Philip and Nina Carmichael, in the crash of a small commuter plane.

But at the time Jade had known nothing of the accident. She'd been lying in a hospital bed in Los Angeles. And even if she had known, had wanted to return to Evan's side, the doctor in charge of her case would have refused to allow her to leave, arguing that such an action would result in the loss of the child she was carrying.

In the end she had suffered a miscarriage anyway, but no one, certainly not Evan, had even known she was pregnant. And during those lonely heartbreaking days as she'd lain in the hospital bed, longing for the comfort of his arms, she'd shed enough tears to sink a battleship.

As the memory of those agonizing days washed over her once more, she felt fresh tears sting her eyes. Hurriedly she blinked them away, glad Evan had his back to her and couldn't see her face.

"My father's not here," Evan repeated as he

turned to her, a glass of brandy in his hand. For the past half hour he'd been dozing in his father's old recliner, too tired to unpack, exhausted after the arduous drive from Portland.

He'd known coming back to Paradise Lake would stir up old memories, memories best forgotten, but when his father had offered him the cabin as a weekend refuge, a place to mull over the problem he was faced with, he'd accepted it gladly.

And when he'd heard the melodic sound of Jade's voice drifting into his mind, he'd told himself he must be dreaming. But she was real and even more beautiful in the flesh than in the dreams he often had of her, dreams that still haunted him.

Her hair, slightly longer now and curling seductively at her shoulders, was the same incredible shade of auburn, reminding him of autumn leaves burnt by the sun. And he noted a new maturity in her face and in her eyes, eyes that held more than a hint of sorrow in their depths.

"Do you know where your father is?" Jade's question cut through his wayward thoughts.

"Portland," he replied before taking a generous sip of brandy.

"Portland!" Jade repeated unable to hide her surprise. "But he always lets me know when he's coming to town. Are you sure?" she asked. She knew Hank was a little eccentric at times, but she couldn't believe he'd driven to town without letting her know.

"Positive," Evan replied. "When I called him at the end of last week he said he'd meet...uh, me there."

"Didn't he come back with you?" she asked.

"No, as a matter of fact, he didn't. He said he had some business to take care of, something to do with the newspaper," Evan added. Hank owned and operated a number of small businesses, including two community newspapers, and he made frequent trips to Portland.

"I see," Jade said, realizing with a pang she'd made the trip to Paradise Lake for nothing. Her godfather was fine—that much was clear—and while she was relieved by the knowledge, she silently promised herself the next time she saw Hank she would give him a piece of her mind.

But on reflection, while it wasn't like Hank not to let her know he'd be in Portland, the fact that he'd arranged to meet Evan there was explanation enough.

Ever since the breakup of her engagement a year ago Jade had refused to discuss the matter with Hank. At first he'd badgered her, wanting to know what had gone wrong, but she'd maintained her silence. In the end he'd stopped asking and adhered to her request not to mention Evan's name.

Slowly it began to sink in that if Hank hadn't made the return trip to Paradise Lake, she was here alone with Evan. Jade's heart gave a quicksilver leap at this thought but she quickly squelched her response, reminding herself that she was over him, that he no longer had the power to hurt her.

"Seems to me you and my father got your wires crossed," Evan remarked, wondering for a moment why his father hadn't simply taken the time to give Jade a quick call from the hotel in Portland.

"I'm just relieved to know he's all right," Jade said. "And now I'd better be on my way."

"You can't be serious?" Evan's tone was incredulous, his eyes glinting sardonically as he studied her over the rim of his glass.

"I think it's best," Jade said evenly, refraining from adding that she'd rather die of exposure than spend a night under the same roof with him.

"I doubt you'll get far." Evan crossed to the window and reached for the cord to open the drapes. "Didn't you hear the storm warning on the radio as you were driving here?"

"Storm warning?" Jade repeated, casting an anxious glance at Evan. The radio in her car wasn't working and she hadn't bothered to get it fixed. And while the steady snowfall had worried her a little, throughout the drive her thoughts had been preoccupied with Hank and what she would find at the cabin.

"You never did like listening to the radio, did you?" Evan remarked with a shake of his head. "Well, if you had been listening you'd know the storm has been upgraded to a blizzard. The I-5 wasn't too bad but the secondary roads were deteriorating rapidly when I got here an hour ago. You were lucky you made it this far."

As he finished speaking, he pulled on the cord and the heavy drapes swung back to reveal a swirling mass of mammoth-size snowflakes falling past the window. In the short time since Jade had brought her car to a halt outside, the storm had worsened considerably.

The lake itself and surrounding hillside had van-

ished behind a curtain of white, and the thick layer
of clouds were heavy with the promise of more
snow. The wind, too, was busy whipping the falling
snowflakes into a frenzy, making it impossible to
see much more than a few inches ahead.

"I'd say *blizzard* is an apt description, wouldn't
you?" Evan commented. "Looks like you'll be
spending the night right here after all."

"But I can't—" Jade burst out in alarm. "I mean,
I have to get back...." She ground to a halt, annoyed
at the panic she could hear in her voice.

Her decision to drive to the cabin had been made
on the spur of the moment after she'd tried calling
Hank from the offices of *Everywoman Magazine,*
where she worked as a freelance writer.

Fearing the worst, she hadn't even bothered to go
home to her apartment but had simply hopped into
her car and headed for the freeway.

Jade avoided looking at Evan, focusing instead on
the snow outside, silently praying for it to stop. But
she knew she was fooling herself, knew that to even
attempt the return journey in these conditions would
be nothing short of suicidal. Evan was right—she'd
been very fortunate to have made to it the cabin at
all.

"Don't be a fool, Jade," Evan said cuttingly.
"You're not going anywhere. I'm afraid you're
stuck here with me—" He stopped abruptly, his
mouth twisting into a bitter smile. "Ah, now I understand the problem," he continued. "You'd rather
freeze to death in the snow than stay here with me.
Is that it?"

"Don't be ridiculous." Jade felt her face grow

warm under the skeptical look in his cool blue eyes. ''I've got to get back.... I have a…a date.'' She stumbled over the words and watched as one dark eyebrow rose mockingly.

''Did you say 'a date'?'' he repeated, his tone mildly curious and faintly derisive.

So what if she was stretching the truth a little? She certainly wasn't about to admit that to Evan. Besides, she did have a date; the fact that it was a lunch date next Tuesday with her friend and boss Veronica Chapman was really none of his business.

''Yes, a date,'' she confirmed, daring to meet his eyes before glancing past to the snow continuing to accumulate at lightning speed on the sundeck.

''Well, I'm afraid your…uh, date…is going to be disappointed, because there's no way you're driving anywhere, at least not tonight,'' Evan said.

Not for the first time since setting out, Jade wished she hadn't been so impulsive, wished she'd held off for another day. If Hank was in Portland as Evan had said, he was probably trying to call her right now. And if she'd gone home first and checked her answering machine she wouldn't be in the awkward predicament of having to stay the night at the cabin.

''You're right,'' Jade reluctantly conceded. ''Excuse me. I left my car running.'' Turning on her heel, she hurried from the room.

A smile tugged at the corner of Evan's mouth as he watched her leave. He'd noted the play of emotions that flitted across her face, emotions ranging from anger to resignation.

During their brief engagement, whenever they'd

gotten into an argument or had a difference of opinion, Jade had hated to acknowledge defeat, at least verbally, and tonight was no exception. Evan's smile widened when he recalled that Jade had found a more beguiling way to let him know he was the victor, usually offering herself as the spoils.

A pain sliced through him at the memory and he cursed under his breath, shaken by the knowledge that she still had the power to affect him. Having Jade turn up was a complication he didn't need.

When his father had suggested he spend the weekend at the cabin, he'd been grateful for the offer, grateful to have a place where he could sit down and plan his strategy. While he knew his lawyer was busy checking out all the legal options, Evan was a man who liked to explore all the angles himself and be well prepared in case of surprises.

If he'd learned anything during his thirty-five years on the planet, it was to expect the unexpected. Fate had thrown him more than his share of curve balls, and one more in the form of the woman he'd never quite been able to get out of his system made no difference. Besides, there was a part of him that was curious what her reaction would be when she found out what had brought him home.

Home…the word and all the images it evoked washed over him, and for a fleeting moment he found himself wishing for the impossible.

"I don't suppose it matters where I sleep, does it?" Jade asked, bringing Evan out of his reverie. Downing the remainder of the brandy in his glass, he turned to face her.

She'd removed her sheepskin jacket and he let his

gaze roam lazily and suggestively over her slender figure. She wore a pair of black stretch pants and a knitted sweater that reached the middle of her thighs and did little to hide the seductive contours of her body. For a mind-numbing moment he wished he could explore more thoroughly and at leisure the changes he could see in her.

"Is that an offer?" he asked, unable to quash the old impulse to tease, remembering how he'd loved to goad her just to watch the hot rush of color suffuse her face.

Jade bristled at his tone. Green eyes flashed temper at him, and until that moment he hadn't truly realized just how much he'd missed seeing the fire in her soul.

"Definitely not!" Jade countered acidly.

"Too bad," Evan responded casually. "I suppose your…date might not approve." While he managed to keep his tone casual, an emotion he instantly recognized as jealousy twisted inside him at the thought of Jade dating another man, kissing another man, making love with another man.

"That's really none of your business," Jade told him.

"You're absolutely right," Evan replied, angry at his reaction and suddenly tired of the banter. "I dropped Ma—" He broke off, ignoring the questioning glance she threw his way. "I'm using the guest suite downstairs," he told her. "Your old room is available if you want it."

"Thank you," she said.

"Now that we have the sleeping arrangements

sorted out, can I offer you a drink?'' Evan asked nonchalantly.

''No, thank you,'' Jade responded. The less time she spent alone with Evan the better. She'd managed to keep busy during the past year and she'd worked hard to cut her memories of Evan out of her mind and her heart. It hadn't been easy.

Her gaze drifted over him for a moment, noticing several changes. He'd lost weight since she'd seen him last—that much was obvious, though somehow it only added to the mystique—giving him a leaner, more athletic appearance. His midnight black hair sported a few gray strands that served to enhance his startling good looks. He was still by far the most attractive man she'd ever known. Just seeing him again set off all kinds of alarm bells inside her.

She turned to leave.

''Jade…wait…''

The sound of her name on his lips sent a quiver of longing racing up her spine. She stopped in the doorway, fighting to ignore the way her pulse stumbled against her throat before gathering speed once more.

''Look…there's something you should know,'' Evan said, having decided it was better to tell her now than wait until morning.

She spun around to face him, and his breath caught in his throat at the look of anger he could see in the depths of her emerald green eyes. ''I'm really not interested in anything you have to say.'' Her words ripped through him, reopening old wounds.

''Touché!'' Evan acknowledged softly, inclining

his head a fraction. He curved his mouth into a smile, unwilling to let her see just how much pain she'd inflicted. "It's a relief to know that your sparring skills remain intact," he added coolly.

A wave of forgotten pleasure danced through Jade. She'd always enjoyed their verbal clashes, clashes that were resolved more often than not beneath the bedcovers.

"It was a long drive and I'm really rather tired," she said, disturbed by the power of the memories tapping at the windows of her mind.

"No problem," Evan replied, wondering if she'd remember in the morning that he had tried to warn her. "Good night," he said before returning to the liquor cabinet.

Jade hesitated in the doorway. Her gaze lingered on the broad expanse of his back, noticing with a guilty pang the way his shoulders seemed to sag. She knew simply by his body language there was something on his mind, and when his hand came up to massage his neck she wished she hadn't snapped at him.

Annoyed at what she perceived as her own weakness she picked up her laptop computer and purse she'd retrieved from her car, not stopping until she reached the bedroom Hank had told her was hers when she'd moved to Paradise Lake at the age of sixteen after her father died.

Hank had been her father's closest friend and he'd helped her deal with her grief, helped her through a very difficult time, never intruding, never patronizing but always there whenever she'd needed a shoulder to cry on.

At the time of her father's death Evan had been on an extended tour of Europe.

As fate or luck would have it, their paths had never crossed, but she'd listened to Hank talk with pride and affection about his son, Evan, and his accomplishments in the field of news reporting.

She'd even studied and secretly admired Evan's handsome figure in the numerous photographs scattered throughout the cabin.

Suddenly the memory of their first meeting and the emotions Evan had aroused with just one kiss threatened to overwhelm her. With grim determination she closed the door on the past, an effort that brought tears to her eyes, tears she angrily brushed away.

As she slowly let her gaze travel around her old room, a pain squeezed her heart. She'd forgotten how much she'd missed the place and the strong sense of home and family she'd always felt whenever she was here. She had Hank to thank for that and that was why she had vowed to always be there for him.

A hot bath would help soothe her fraught nerves, she decided, but it wasn't until she climbed from the tub and wrapped herself in the bath towel that she realized she had no nightdress, no clothes except for those she'd arrived in.

Muttering under her breath, Jade returned to her room and rummaged through her old chest of drawers in the hope of unearthing a T-shirt, anything that might be deemed suitable to use as night attire.

But apart from a drawer filled with some of her old bulky knit sweaters and another with wool socks and a couple of pairs of faded blue jeans, she found nothing even resembling a nightshirt.

With a sigh of frustration Jade tugged the towel around her and opened her bedroom door. All she had to do, she assured herself, was to sneak downstairs to Hank's bedroom and borrow one of his shirts.

She tiptoed down the hallway, stopping at the top of the stairs to listen for Evan. All was quiet. Just as she reached the last few steps she heard a door open, followed by the sound of footsteps. It was too late to turn and make a dash for the upper landing.

Evan stopped when he saw her. "Planning to surprise me, were you? Changed your mind about where you're sleeping?" Evan's tone was laced with humor as his gaze swept over her half-naked body.

"Absolutely not!" Jade retorted, tightening her hold on the towel and feeling the color rush to her cheeks. Silently she chastised herself for acting on impulse. "I didn't...I mean, I should have..." She ground to a halt as she watched one dark eyebrow rise fractionally while his mouth twitched in what might have been a smile. "I left in rather a hurry and didn't stop to pack an overnight bag," she explained.

"Oh...I see," Evan answered, fighting the urge to reach out and tug the edge of the towel free of her white-knuckled grip. "Want to borrow one of my shirts?" he asked. "It'll be like old times," he added, recalling vividly how most mornings during their four months together she'd emerge from the bathroom looking incredibly sexy wearing one of his shirts.

"Thank you," Jade managed to reply, ignoring the shiver of excitement that shimmied down her spine at his fleeting reference to the past.

"Don't go away," Evan instructed before sauntering down the dimly lit hallway.

As she waited Jade found herself wondering why Evan had chosen to occupy the guest suite instead of his old bedroom upstairs, but curious as she was to know the answer, she decided not to pose the question.

Evan returned in less than a minute, a pale blue, long-sleeved shirt in his hand.

"Your nightshirt, *madam,*" he said with a grin as he held the article out to her.

It was all Jade could do not to snatch the shirt from him. "Thank you," she muttered through gritted teeth. Avoiding his eyes, she turned on her heels and scurried up the stairs, aware every step of the way that Evan was watching her.

Tossing the towel on her bed, Jade slid her arms into Evan's shirt and buttoned it up. In an instant she was bombarded with the familiar scent of lime and leather, mixed with the stronger, more potent smell of pure unadulterated male.

A kaleidoscope of memories flashed unbidden into her head and with a choked cry she began to unbutton the shirt. A sudden gust of wind rattled the shutters on the window and Jade's fingers stilled in their task.

With trembling fingers she rebuttoned the shirt and, crossing to the bed under the window she slipped beneath the covers.

Lying in the darkness she listened to the wind

howling outside, to the creaks and groans coming from the cabin. Resolutely she told herself she didn't want to know what had brought Evan here or what was troubling him. It wasn't any of her business and she really didn't care.

She would leave early in the morning and return to Portland and this brief little encounter would soon be forgotten. But she couldn't seem to silence the little voice inside her head insisting she was only fooling herself.

Jade drifted off into a dreamless sleep and was awakened by the sound of the shutter banging against the window. Rolling over, she glanced at the small clock on the bedside table. It was two in the morning.

Snuggling under the covers once more, she tried to go back to sleep, but it wasn't long before her stomach began to protest loudly that it hadn't been fed for quite some time.

Jade berated herself for not stopping for a bite to eat. But in her hurry to assure herself Hank was all right, food had been the last thing on her mind.

She hadn't eaten since earlier in the afternoon, and that had only been a muffin and coffee. Her stomach rumbled again in noisy reminder. She was starving!

Pushing the covers aside, she sat up in bed, contemplating the options. She could either wait until breakfast or raid the fridge now.

Out in the darkened hallway she listened for a sound that would tell her Evan was still up and about, but this time she was met with the heavy sound of silence.

Jade didn't bother to turn on the light. As she padded down the hall, the hardwood floor felt as cold as a block of ice. Her plan was simple—make herself a peanut butter sandwich, pour a glass of milk, then take the spoils upstairs to her room. She'd done it hundreds of times over the years.

At the foot of the stairs she threw a quick cursory glance down the hallway leading to the guest suite. She held her breath for a moment but all she could hear was the wind buffeting outside.

Slipping quietly into the kitchen, she switched on the light and crossed to the counter. When she opened the cupboard door she spotted several jars of peanut butter on the shelf and murmured a thank-you to Hank for keeping a stock of her favorite brand.

Her mouth began to water in anticipation and she quickly located a loaf of bread in the wooden bread box on the counter.

Fearful Evan might hear her shuffling around and come to investigate, Jade wasted no time in making the sandwich. After pouring herself a glass of milk, she turned to leave.

''Can I have one, too?'' a small voice asked.

Jade felt her heart slam against her breastbone in startled reaction, and she almost dropped the glass of milk she was holding. Her gaze flew to the doorway and she found herself staring at a sleepy-eyed, dark-haired boy of about seven. His eyes were almost as blue as Evan's.

Chapter Two

"Who are you?" Jade asked.

"Matthew," said the boy. "Who are you?"

Jade blinked several times and drew a deep, steadying breath. "Uh, my name is Jade," she responded, continuing to stare at the child dressed only in a T-shirt and underpants and wearing no slippers. His eyes, she noticed now, were more gray than blue, and the hint of sadness she could see in their depths tugged at her heart.

"Are you going to eat that?" Matthew asked, a hopeful expression on his small face.

"Uh, well…" Jade glanced at the sandwich, then back at the child, whose gaze was focused on the bread in her hand. "It's a peanut butter sandwich. Would you like one?"

"Yes, please" came the prompt reply followed by a heartwarming smile.

"Why don't you have this one?" she offered.

"And the milk, too." Jade set the sandwich and the glass of milk on the kitchen table. She caught the flicker of uncertainty in the boy's eyes. "It's all right," she assured him. "I'll make myself another."

"Oh…okay," Matthew said before scrambling eagerly onto one of the kitchen chairs.

Jade watched him take a bite of the sandwich followed by a gulp of milk that left a white mustache. Whose child was he? she wondered. Evan's? Her heart skipped a beat, but she instantly dismissed the notion. A more likely explanation was the probability that Matthew's mother was Evan's new love interest. And perhaps that new love interest was at this moment lying in Evan's arms.

Pain and confusion clouded her vision for a moment. Was that what Evan had wanted to tell her earlier? That he'd brought a woman with him?

"Can I have another one?" Matthew's question cut through Jade's musing.

"Oh…sure." She returned to the counter and made two sandwiches, all the while trying to come to terms with the fact that Evan might not be alone. "Would you like more milk?" she asked, setting a second sandwich in front of the boy.

Her question was met with a nod. Jade refilled his glass and poured one for herself. Pulling out a chair, she sat down opposite Matthew and for several minutes they ate in companionable silence.

"I hope I didn't wake you when I came downstairs," Jade said, her curiosity finally getting the better of her.

Matthew shook his head and took another bite of his sandwich.

"You must have been really hungry." She smiled as his tongue came out to lick a streak of peanut butter from his fingers. "Is that why you woke up?"

This time he nodded.

"I guess you didn't want to wake your mother," Jade continued, knowing she was probing but hoping Matthew might simply volunteer the information she was after. To her dismay his eyes filled with tears and his lower lip began to quiver.

"His mother's dead." Evan's softly spoken words exploded like a bomb into the tense silence. Jade's glance darted to where he stood in the doorway, and her heart went into an instant tailspin at the sight of him, his hair tousled from sleep, his chest bare, the top button of his cords undone as if he'd leapt out of bed and hurriedly pulled them on.

Matthew dropped the partially eaten sandwich onto the table and, hopping down from the chair, ran to the man who'd just joined them. Mesmerized, Jade watched as Evan scooped the boy into his arms and Matthew buried his face against Evan's broad shoulder and began to cry. Her breath caught in her throat at the look of love and concern in Evan's expression.

"I see you've met Matthew," he said.

Jade swallowed the lump of emotion clogging her throat. "Yes," she managed to say, entranced by the way Evan was gently stroking the child's head and murmuring words of comfort in his ear.

All at once a thought exploded like a firecracker inside Jade's head. Had their baby lived, had she carried Evan's child to full term, their son or daughter would have been three months old now.

The spasm of pain that knifed through Jade caught her off guard and it was all she could do to stifle the moan of anguish gathering in her throat. She put her hand to her mouth, fearful Evan would notice her distress. Rising from the table, she picked up the half-empty glasses and the forgotten sandwiches and turned to the sink.

She knew firsthand the agony of losing a parent. She'd been ten when her own mother died and she'd lost her father when she was sixteen. Behind her she could hear Matthew's soft whimpering cries, and fresh feelings of guilt washed over her. The need to comfort the child suddenly overwhelmed her.

Reining in her own emotions, Jade turned. "I'm so sorry, Matthew. I didn't mean to upset you," she said.

Matthew didn't respond. Evan met and held her gaze and she noted with a start the look of intense sorrow lurking there.

"Matthew knows that, don't you, buddy?" Evan spoke gently to the boy and Matthew nodded in acknowledgment, though he didn't turn around. "He'll be okay," Evan assured her. "I'd better put him back to bed."

After they'd gone, Jade returned to the sink and rinsed the glasses, pondering on the look she'd seen in Evan's eyes. She'd been right about his having something on his mind, and the fact that it centered around Matthew was obvious. But Jade couldn't quite figure out just what Evan's connection was to the boy, nor did she understand why he'd brought Matthew to Paradise Lake.

Whatever the reason, it was none of her business, she reminded herself as she put the knife in the drawer.

"I didn't think you'd still be here." When he'd noticed the light still on in the kitchen, he'd assumed Jade had forgotten to switch it off. He hadn't expected to find her there, nor had he expected to find that look of pain and sadness on her face.

Evan's voice effectively cut through her wayward thoughts. Jade tensed and chastised herself for not escaping upstairs when she had the chance. "I was just tidying up." She dropped the dish towel onto the counter and, conscious of the fact she wore only the shirt Evan had given her earlier, she turned to leave. But her exit was barred.

She halted a few feet in front of him and her gaze was instantly drawn to the breastplate of fine dark hairs on his muscled chest. Her mouth went dry and her pulse kicked into high gear.

"I tried to tell you about Matthew," Evan said.

Jade moistened her lips with the tip of her tongue. "I realize that now," she responded.

"In case you're wondering, Matthew is Nina and Philip's son," Evan told her.

Jade glanced up at him, understanding now the sorrow she'd seen in him. "I'd forgotten they had a little boy," she said. Then she quickly added, "He wasn't on the plane with them, was he?"

Evan shook his head. "They'd left Matthew with some friends. He had an ear infection and the doctor told them it wasn't a good idea for him to fly."

"How awful for him…to lose both parents like that." Jade spoke softly.

"It's been tough for him, all right." Evan managed to keep his voice even. "And more than any child should have to endure," he went on, emotion seeping into his words. "But he's quite the little trouper."

"It must have been awful for you, too, Evan," Jade said. "You lost your best friends. I can't tell you how sorry I was to hear of the crash," she went on, knowing her words were both inadequate and somewhat late, yet wanting to say them just the same.

Evan held her gaze for a long moment, staring deeply into her eyes almost as if he was searching for something—she knew not what. The air between them was suddenly alive with tension, and she curled her fingers into tight fists to stop herself from reaching up to smooth away the lines of worry she could see on his forehead.

"Why didn't you come to the funeral?" Evan asked abruptly, and there was no mistaking the reproach in his voice.

Jade stiffened. "You'd just broken off our engagement, remember?" she responded icily, silently adding that she hadn't learned about the crash of the small commuter plane or the deaths of Evan's friends Nina and Philip until a few days after it happened.

That was because on her arrival in Los Angeles an ambulance had whisked her to the nearest hospital, where she'd spent three days fighting for the life of their unborn child and another three recovering from a miscarriage.

"I remember only too well," Evan said with a tired sigh. "I just thought—" He broke off abruptly. "Look, thanks for making a sandwich for Matthew." He hurried on in a swift and deliberate change of subject. "Neither of us ate much today, and with the traveling we've been doing these past few days, I thought Matthew needed sleep more than he needed food. I guess I was wrong."

"No problem," Jade replied. For a moment she was tempted to ask him why he'd brought Matthew with him to Paradise Lake, why Matthew was with him at all, but she bit back the questions, reminding herself that it was really no concern of hers.

"Jade?" Her name on his lips was a softly spoken question, effectively cutting through her wandering thoughts.

She glanced up at him, and for a heart-stopping second she was catapulted back in time to the night he'd kissed her for the very first time, the night he'd stolen her heart. She remembered feeling the same breathless tension, the same tingling awareness and the same dizzying sensation moments before his mouth claimed hers.

As Evan gazed into the bejeweled depths of Jade's eyes he was amazed to discover he wanted quite desperately to haul her into his arms and lose himself in her sweetness and warmth. But tempted as he was to sip again from the elixir of her lips, he held himself rigidly in check, knowing from past experience one sip would neither satisfy nor diminish the need she could arouse in him, and knowing, too, when he'd broken their engagement a year ago, he'd tossed away his chance of finding happiness.

"You'd better get some rest. You'll want to be fresh for the drive back to Portland tomorrow," he said, effectively defusing the tension arcing between them. "See you at breakfast." With that he turned and left.

Several long moments passed before Jade could make herself move. For a timeless second she'd thought Evan was going to kiss her and she knew without a shadow of a doubt she would have kissed him back. Fool! She berated herself. Hadn't she learned her lesson?

Taking a deep steadying breath, Jade crossed to the doorway, switched off the kitchen light and headed for the stairs. Back in her room she lay beneath the bedcovers, staring into the darkness, listening to the wind whistling outside and telling herself repeatedly she was completely and totally over Evan, that what she'd felt for him hadn't been love at all but only infatuation.

She was a year older and much wiser now. He'd taught her a valuable lesson, never to give her heart so freely or so willingly. Surely she wouldn't be foolish enough to make the same mistake again?

"Are you awake?"

At the sound of the strange voice Jade struggled from the realms of sleep to find herself staring into the face of a small boy. Startled, she blinked several times, sure she must be dreaming, then all at once the events of the previous evening came rushing back.

"Matthew," she said sleepily. "Good morning. How are you today?" Jade slowly eased herself into a sitting position.

"Okay," he said, his gaze traveling around the room.

"Have you had breakfast?" she asked, wondering if Evan had sent Matthew upstairs to waken her.

He shook his head. "Evan's making toast," he said.

"Really," Jade commented dryly, all the while thinking Evan's cooking skills hadn't improved much since she'd last seen him. "Is it still snowing?" She glanced toward the window.

"Yup" came the prompt reply. "Evan says there's enough snow outside to make a zillion snowmen," Matthew continued excitedly.

Jade swallowed a groan. She'd hoped the snow had miraculously disappeared overnight. Pushing back the covers, she rose from the bed and crossed to the window. She tugged hard on the roll-up blind, and as it retracted, she had to scrunch up her eyes at the sudden and startling brightness.

"Oh…" she exclaimed, and gazed in awe at the sight before her. Her bedroom window overlooked the rear of the property, and for as far as the eye could see, it looked as if an enormous thick, white, fluffy quilt had been spread over the ground.

At the foot of the garden a line of tall cedar trees, their branches sagging from the weight of the snow, stood like white sentinels guarding a fairy-tale world.

Tiny snowflakes floated from the cloud-filled sky, adding a fresh layer to what Jade felt sure had to be a record snowfall. ''Rats and mice!'' she muttered under her breath, annoyed at Mother Nature's incredibly bad timing.

''Where?'' Matthew asked, peering out of the window.

''What?'' Jade replied, frowning at him.

''Where are the rats and mice?'' Matthew asked innocently. ''I don't see any.''

Jade smiled and shook her head. ''No...there aren't any,'' she told him. ''I say that when I'm annoyed,'' she explained as her gaze swept over the pristine landscape once more.

''What are you annoyed at?'' Matthew asked.

''The snow,'' she replied.

''The snow? But it looks neat,'' Matthew stated brightly.

Jade glanced down at the boy standing beside her, noting the expression of wide-eyed wonder in his blue-gray eyes. Playfully she ruffled his hair and smiled. ''To you, I suppose it does,'' she responded, pondering for a moment on the problem of just how she was going to get her car down the driveway and onto the main road.

''Want to help me and Evan build a snowman?'' Matthew asked. ''We can make snow angels, too. I know how,'' he assured her.

''Matthew! What are you doing in Jade's bedroom?'' The deep timbre of Evan's voice startled both Jade and Matthew, and together they spun around to see Evan's tall, imposing figure standing in the doorway.

Jade's heart did a familiar somersault inside her breast. The sight of Evan in a pair of snug-fitting blue jeans and a white polo-necked sweater, his hair still wet from the shower, his jaw clean-shaven and inviting, brought a rush of old memories crowding in on her.

Beside her Matthew lowered his chin onto his chest and gazed sheepishly at Evan. ''I was just exploring,'' he explained. ''You said I could,'' he dared to add.

''Ah, exploring,'' Evan repeated, and Jade felt her pulse gather speed when she saw the glint of amusement dancing in his eyes. ''You're right, I did say you could explore. But I told you to stay downstairs.''

''I know….but I finished exploring down there,'' Matthew was quick to point out. ''And I just wanted to see if she was awake.'' He stopped and threw Jade an apologetic glance.

''Her name is Jade. And it's rude to enter someone's bedroom, especially a lady's, without an invitation,'' Evan scolded gently. ''I hope he didn't wake you,'' he added, shifting his attention to Jade.

''No, he didn't wake me,'' Jade quickly assured him, feeling her cheeks grow warm under his steady gaze.

''Okay, sport, your breakfast is ready,'' Evan said, wishing now he hadn't set out in search of the boy. The sight of Jade in one of his shirts, her auburn hair in a state of riotous disarray, was having an adverse effect on his blood pressure. ''There's hot cereal and toast waiting for you downstairs. Let's give Jade some privacy, shall we?''

Matthew threw Jade another apologetic smile before he scooted past Evan into the hallway.

"Coffee's on. By the time you come downstairs it'll be ready," he informed Jade before withdrawing and closing the door behind him.

Jade slowly released the breath she'd been holding. For the past few minutes she'd been achingly aware of Evan's gaze raking over her and annoyed at just how vulnerable and exposed he'd made her feel.

Her reaction seemed foolish, to say the least. After all, they'd become lovers on the night he'd slipped a beautiful emerald and diamond ring on her finger only a scant two weeks after that first fateful and unforgettable meeting.

Evan had been a masterful lover, unlocking the sensual secrets of her body with infinite patience, teaching her the joys of intimacy with a tender urgency that had left her breathless and totally fulfilled.

A shudder chased through her as a cavalcade of forgotten sensations darted across her nerve endings, awakening yearnings she'd thought were carefully locked away. Resolutely Jade slammed the door on the memories clamoring to resurface and headed for the bathroom.

After a quick shower she dressed in a pair of her old blue jeans and a baggy sweatshirt she found in the drawer. Brushing her hair into a ponytail, she tied it loosely with a yellow scarf that accented the rich color of her hair.

She retrieved a pair of heavy wool socks from the dresser and used them for slippers. As she descended the stairs her heart suddenly picked up speed and the familiar sensation of a thousand butterfly wings fluttering in her stomach assailed her.

A sense of déjà vu brought her to a halt. This was exactly how she'd felt the morning after Evan had kissed her for the very first time. She'd been a mass of contradictions then, torn between the longing to see him again and assure herself she hadn't simply dreamed the kiss they'd shared, and wondering if he'd tell her it had all been a big mistake and he regretted what had taken place between them.

Jade silently scolded herself. She was no longer the naive girl who'd been engaged to Evan. She'd grown up a lot since then. She'd had to.

Besides, Evan hadn't kissed her last night, and if she wanted proof he'd never really loved her, all she had to do was recall the unfeeling way he'd broken their engagement and along with it her heart.

Stiffening her spine, Jade banished the butterflies and strode with confidence toward the kitchen. The enticing scent of freshly brewed coffee greeted her as she entered, and Matthew threw her a welcoming smile when he glanced up from his bowl of cereal.

"The coffee smells wonderful," she said, thinking if it tasted as good as the aroma promised, Evan had obviously developed a few domestic skills since she'd last seen him.

"Sit down. I'll bring you a cup," Evan said, turning from the sink.

"Thank you. I'll help myself." Jade crossed to where the coffeemaker sat on the counter. She filled a mug and brought it to her lips. "Mmm…this is really good," she told him.

"Don't sound so surprised." Evan threw her an amused glance.

Jade met his gaze head-on. "If memory serves me well, boiling water to make instant coffee was your only claim to fame in the culinary department," she declared, a hint of a challenge in her tone.

"True…very true," he conceded as he spread jam on a piece of toast. "But I seem to recall your telling me on numerous occasions that I more than made up for it in other areas."

His eyes blazed a silent message as they met hers, and Jade felt a hot rush of color suffuse her face at the implication behind his words. She glared at him over the rim of the mug, sorely tempted to toss the remainder of her coffee at him, but the glint of humor she could see in his expression told her he knew exactly what she was contemplating.

Turning away, she gulped down a mouthful of coffee, almost scalding herself in the process, but she was determined Evan wouldn't see the answering smile tugging insistently at the corners of her mouth.

Damn the man! He'd always had an uncanny knack of pushing the right buttons where she was concerned. She'd reacted out of habit, that was all.

"How's breakfast, Matthew?" Jade asked, intent on distracting her thoughts. She pulled out the chair opposite Matthew and sat down. "Is it safe to eat?" she asked him. At her question she heard Evan's low chuckle, a sound that sent her pulse skipping crazily.

"Uh-huh…it's good," Matthew reported. "It's cimm…cinn…cimmamum flavored." He tripped over the pronunciation and Jade had to hide her smile.

"It comes in a package. You just add hot water," Evan told her before she could comment. He held up the box of cereal. "If that doesn't tempt you, I could scramble up a few eggs," he offered.

Jade raised her eyebrows and regarded him with a look of skepticism. Throughout their four months together he had never once cooked for her, never made as much as a sandwich. In the rather nomadic existence he'd lived for most of his working life, he'd formed the habit of relying on hotel restaurants or cafés, grabbing meals on the run.

"No thanks. I'll just have toast," she said, pushing back her chair.

"Ask and you shall receive," Evan countered. He came up behind her and brought his hand down on her shoulder to prevent her from rising. "Lightly buttered, just the way you like it." With a flourish he set a plate with two slices of toast on the place mat in front of her.

"Oh...thank you," she managed to mutter, glancing up at him. Beneath his hand her skin tingled in heady response to his casual touch.

"Can I have more juice, please?" Matthew asked.

"Coming right up," Evan said, moving away. He crossed to the fridge, allowing Jade a few moments to regain control of her scattered senses. "Would you care for a glass of orange juice?" he asked as he refilled Matthew's glass.

"Uh, no thanks," Jade replied. She picked up a piece of toast and found her thoughts drifting back to the mornings she'd awakened to find herself alone with a note on the pillow beside her saying he'd see her later or he'd call.

She'd tried to be patient, tried not to resent the fact that his work obviously came first, but it hadn't been easy. After all, she'd been the one who'd insisted on dropping out of her last year at college in order to travel with him and be by his side.

Both Evan and Hank had been opposed to her decision, but she'd been deeply in love and determined to prove to herself and to Evan that although she was twelve years younger than her handsome fiancé, she was more than capable of taking on the various roles that came under the heading of wife.

What she'd been unwilling to admit either to herself or to Evan was her fear that Evan might grow tired of her and regret asking her to marry him. In the end, she'd been right and her worst fears had indeed come to pass.

"Want to come outside and help me and Evan build a snowman?" Matthew's voice cut through Jade's wayward thoughts, bringing her attention back to the present.

"That sounds like fun, Matthew," she began. "But I'm driving back to Portland this morning," she explained, softening her refusal with a smile.

"You must be joking!" Evan glared at her from behind Matthew's chair.

Jade bristled at his tone. "I said I'd leave in the morning—that's still my plan," she responded.

"You did look outside, didn't you?" Evan asked. "Surely you noticed that a lot more snow fell during the night," he commented. "It's my guess the secondary roads are closed and they'll stay that way until this storm blows over. And if the clouds gathering outside are anything to go by, that won't be anytime soon.''

"But surely if I get to the main road..." Jade protested.

"And just how do you propose to do that?" Evan challenged. "Does your car have wings?"

"But I have to leave," Jade insisted, trying not to sound petulant.

"That's what you said last night," Evan said, eyeing her with some disdain. "He must really be someone special, this date of yours," he commented dryly. "My advice to you is to give him a call and tell him you won't be able to make it." He turned to the boy, who'd been silently watching their exchange with wide-eyed interest.

"Matthew, if you're through with breakfast, why don't you go and put on the snow pants and ski jacket I bought for you the other day? We have a snowman to build. Right?"

"Right!" the boy eagerly agreed. Jumping down from the chair, Matthew headed toward the door.

"Don't forget your gloves and hat," Evan called after the departing figure.

"I still think if I can get out to the main road I'll be fine," Jade said with more confidence than she was feeling, stubbornly determined to prove him wrong.

Evan threw her a scathing look and shook his head. "There's no law against trying, I suppose," he said with a sigh. "I'd offer to help dig your car out if I thought there was even the slightest chance you'd make it. But I can't see the point of wasting energy on such a futile exercise. Excuse me. I'd better see if Matthew needs any help.''

Alone in the kitchen, Jade rose from the chair, crossed to the window and pulled a face at the snowflakes falling with steady monotony to the ground.

Jade knew Evan was right, knew she'd never get her car turned around, let alone down the driveway, but if the truth be known, her reluctance to stay stemmed solely from the fact she was stranded here with him.

Seeing Evan again had affected her more deeply than she was willing to admit. And while Matthew's presence had reawakened the painful memory of losing her own child, she couldn't bring herself to resent Matthew, not after all he'd been through.

Poor Matthew. Evan was right, he was a brave little boy. That he'd forgiven her for her tactless remarks the previous night was obvious, but she was still at a loss to understand why Matthew was here with Evan.

The explanation was no doubt a simple one. Perhaps Evan was on vacation and he'd invited Matthew along. It didn't surprise her in the least that Evan had remained in close contact with Philip and Nina's son.

She and Evan had talked about starting a family of their own. Evan had seemed reticent about the idea, telling her they had plenty of time, pointing out that raising a child required a great deal of effort and energy, adding his belief that children needed a solid and stable environment in which to grow.

While Jade had agreed with him on two of the points, she hadn't wanted to wait. She'd longed for a baby—Evan's baby—believing with all her heart Evan would be a fabulous father. Seeing him with Matthew, watching the way he'd held and comforted the boy last night confirmed she was right.

Not for the first time Jade wondered what Evan's reaction would have been if he'd known about her pregnancy. When the doctor at the hospital in L.A. had told her the intermittent pains she'd been experiencing throughout the flight from New Orleans were consistent with a possible miscarriage, she'd been stunned to learn she was carrying Evan's child.

Over a period of a few days the pains had gradually begun to diminish, and she'd thought her prayers had been answered. But she'd started hemorrhaging, and later that third day she'd lost the baby.

During her recovery she'd thought long and hard about her relationship with Evan, coming to the realization she'd been foolish to think that someone so young and lacking in sophistication could hold on to a man as worldly as him.

Jade brushed a stray tear from her cheek and resolutely clamped down on the memories threatening to overwhelm her. Focusing once more on the snow outside, she shivered anew, noticing that the flakes seemed larger than before; there was little sign of the storm letting up.

Mumbling under her breath she crossed to the telephone, but just as she reached for the receiver Evan appeared in the doorway.

"I'm afraid you won't be able to contact your lover boy after all," Evan said.

"Why not?" Jade asked, annoyed at his tone.

"I heard on the radio the phone lines are down. Power is out all over the place," he informed her. "Dad mentioned he'd put a new generator in last winter—that's probably why we still have electricity. But that's not the worst of it," he went on.

"What do you mean?" Jade asked, her heart dropping to her toes.

"According to the latest weather report, this storm is building force and is going to be with us for another day, maybe two," he said. "And if you think I'm going to let you try to leave in these conditions, you're very much mistaken. I suggest you accept the fact you're stuck here until the storm blows over."

Chapter Three

Evan watched Jade's face as he imparted the news and saw the flash of annoyance and another emotion, one he couldn't readily define, that came and went in her green eyes.

"There's always skis, I suppose," he said.

"Skis?" Jade responded, her expression quizzical.

"It's just that you seem rather anxious to leave," Evan said. "Are you sure it isn't the thought of being stranded here with me?" he commented dryly.

"Of course not," Jade replied, though she avoided meeting his eyes.

"Didn't you tell your…date…where you were going?" he asked. He knew he was pushing but he couldn't let the subject drop.

Jade bristled at his words and met his steely gaze. "My date happens to be my boss," she was forced to confess.

"Really," Evan said, and watched with some satisfaction as color slowly invaded her cheeks. "And how do you like working for Veronica Chapman? I must say that magazine of hers has improved since you started writing for it."

Jade blinked in astonishment. "But how——?" She broke off. "Hank told you, I suppose," she reasoned aloud, disappointed to learn her godfather had discussed her with Evan.

"No, as a matter of fact, he didn't." Evan quickly set her straight. "My father refused to answer any questions I asked concerning you."

"If Hank didn't tell you, how did you know I was working for the magazine?" she asked more curious than ever.

"Because I made a point of finding out," Evan was swift to reply.

Startled at his words, Jade met his challenging gaze head-on. "I'm surprised you bothered," she countered, her tone bordering on sarcastic.

Evan's mouth tightened into a thin line. "I bothered…because for some perverse reason I wanted to make sure you were all right," he told her tersely. "That was quite the disappearing act," he went on. "But what with the plane crash and learning about Philip and Nina…well, it took me almost a month to track you down." He paused. "I never thought for one moment you'd head to the airport and get on a plane."

"Why not? You broke our engagement, remember? There was really no reason for me to stay." Jade kept a firm grip on her emotions, surprised that even after a year the pain of his rejection still lingered.

When he'd told her he thought they should postpone their wedding indefinitely, that he was having second thoughts and wasn't ready to settle down and give up his nomadic life-style or his freedom, she'd been stunned. All that registered was that her worst fear—he'd grow tired of her—had indeed come to pass.

It was the very first time she hadn't argued with him, teased him or cajoled him into changing his mind. His tone had been much too serious, his rejection much too shattering. Instead, she'd pulled off her engagement ring, calmly placed it on the coffee table and left.

Evan's mouth tightened into a thin line. ''Look, Jade, I know—''

But before he could say more, Matthew appeared, wearing navy blue snow pants and a matching jacket and carrying a pair of gloves and a woollen hat.

''I'm ready. Can we go outside now?'' the boy asked.

Evan summoned a smile. ''Sure,'' he said, suppressing a sigh. ''I'll have to wear an old pair of my father's snow boots. They should be in the closet by the front door. Let's take a look, shall we?''

Matthew threw Jade a friendly glance. ''You can still change your mind and come with us.''

At any other time and in any other circumstances Jade knew she would have readily agreed, but she was determined to keep her distance from Evan. ''Thanks, Matthew, but I have some work to do,'' she said, softening her refusal with a smile.

"What kind of work?" Matthew asked.

"I write for a magazine," Jade explained. "And I have to finish a piece I've been working on."

"Couldn't you do it later?" Matthew persisted.

"Matthew, she said she was too busy," Evan reminded him gently. "Come on, we'll have fun on our own."

A look of disappointment crossed the boy's features, and as she watched Matthew and Evan leave, it was all she could do not to go after them.

Crossing to the coffeepot, Jade refilled her mug, then made her way upstairs. She felt more than a little battered emotionally by the exchange with Evan in the kitchen; she was still trying to deal with the fact that not only had he tracked her down, he'd obviously been keeping tabs on her.

Setting her mug on the bedside table, Jade made her bed then propped her laptop computer on the desk next to the door. She retrieved her coffee and, tapping at the keys, soon brought up the article on sexual harassment in the workplace she'd been working on.

But as she gazed at the words on the screen, her mind refused to concentrate on the task at hand and her thoughts were soon drifting back to the magical and unforgettable weekend Evan had wooed and won her heart.

Working at a summer job as a waitress, she'd traded shifts with a friend and wrangled a much-needed weekend off. She'd thrown some clothes into a bag and headed for Paradise Lake to relax and recharge her batteries.

After the taxi dropped her at the cabin she'd hurried inside, eager to surprise Hank. Only, she'd been the one caught totally and completely by surprise when she'd found herself face-to-face with Evan.

It hadn't taken her but a second to decide the photographs of Evan she'd admired for so long didn't even begin to do justice to the real flesh-and-blood man before her.

His eyes were the exact color of the deepest part of the lake, and his body was, quite simply, to die for. Her heart had started dancing a jig at the sight of him standing in front of the big bay window looking magnificent and godlike in a skimpy black bathing suit.

A strange and unfamiliar sensation had unfurled in the pit of her stomach and a tingling heat had sprinted like wildfire through her veins. For a moment she'd had the distinct impression she was standing on the bow of a small sailboat being tossed about by enormous waves.

"Hello." His eyes had lit up with interest and appreciation. "It's Jade, isn't it? How nice to finally meet you."

She'd had to swallow several times to alleviate the sudden dryness in her throat.

"Hello, yourself," she'd managed to respond, pleased she sounded nonchalant when in reality she was a jumble of jittery nerves.

"Hank's not here. He's gone into Roseburg to stay with friends for the weekend," Evan told her. "He didn't tell me you were coming. I guess he forgot."

"He didn't forget. He didn't know," Jade said.

"It was a spur-of-the-moment decision. I thought I'd surprise him."

"I was just going for a swim. You're welcome to join me," he offered as he reached for the towel hanging on a chair nearby.

"Uh, okay, sure." The words came out in a breathless whisper. She continued to stare at him, fascinated by the play of muscles across his broad chest and inexorably drawn to the sprinkling of fine dark hairs descending in a V shape past his flat stomach to disappear beneath the waistband of his swimsuit.

"Perhaps you should change first," Evan suggested, amusement lacing his voice.

Heat suffused her face, and as she lifted her head to meet his gaze, her breath froze in her throat as she watched his mouth curve into a dazzling smile.

"Yes…change…right." She stopped and bit down on her lower lip to stifle the moan of self-reproach at her staccato answers.

"Great. I'll see you out there." Turning, he headed for the sliding door leading onto the sun-deck.

Jade stood gazing at Evan's departing figure for ten long seconds, mesmerized by the sheer physical beauty of his body. She'd seen men in bathing suits before but the sight of them had never affected her like this.

Her skin prickled, her pulse raced and her lungs appeared to have forgotten how to function. All at once her breath escaped in a soft whistle of appreciation.

Spinning around, she raced upstairs to her room

at breakneck speed, tripping over herself in her
haste, silently praying she hadn't forgotten to pack
the two-piece bathing suit her friend and college
roommate had brought back from a trip she'd taken
to Honolulu during the winter break.

When she joined Evan in the water ten minutes
later she knew it would be an afternoon she
wouldn't soon forget. She spent an inordinate
amount of time lounging on the floating wharf, cov-
ertly admiring Evan's tanned and taut body as he
stroked effortlessly through the water or lazed
nearby.

Her fingers had itched to feel the texture of his
skin and trace the outline of those strong muscular
shoulders. She couldn't seem to stop wondering
what it would feel like to have his body pressed
urgently against hers, or taste the promise of passion
she could see in the sensuous curve of his lips.

Her fantasy became a startling reality later that
same evening, and from the moment his mouth
touched hers, Jade knew nothing in her life would
ever be the same. She was totally unprepared for the
avalanche of emotions sweeping over her or for the
explosion of sensations, the overwhelming outpour-
ing of need that sent her pulse skyrocketing.

His kiss left her weak and trembling, exhilarated
and dizzy all at the same time and she was almost
sure she felt Cupid's arrow pierce her heart as she
surrendered to his mouth's ardent and urgent de-
mands.

Suddenly the sound of a child's squeal of delight
shattered the stillness, jolting Jade out of her reverie.

A ripple of forgotten need vibrated through her and she cursed under her breath for allowing a memory she'd thought was safely tucked away in that secret corner of her heart to escape and awaken old longings.

Rising, she crossed to the window, where her gaze alighted on the twosome below. An involuntary smile warmed her face as she watched Evan and Matthew in the throes of a friendly snowball fight.

Matthew was helping himself from a small stack of snowballs near the foot of the large snowman they'd built. He could scarcely throw the missiles fast enough as Evan kept up a steady barrage from a few feet away.

Bewitched by the grin of mischief on Evan's face, Jade watched as, out of ammunition, he made a run at Matthew in a surprise attack that sent them both sprawling. Side by side they lay sprawled out on the snow, the sound of their shared laughter echoing in the morning stillness.

A pain twisted inside Jade as she watched them. That Evan cared deeply for the boy was written on his handsome features, and fresh tears gathered in Jade's eyes when she thought of the child she'd loved and lost. Evan's child.

Matthew flopped back onto the snow and began to sweep his arms and legs to form a snow angel. He looked up and, spotting Jade, immediately smiled and waved.

Evan followed the boy's gaze, but as their glances collided, the warmth and sparkle evident on his features quickly faded.

A shiver danced across Jade's nerve endings,

leaving behind an icy chill. She waved back before retreating into the room, once more silently admonishing herself for wishing the smile she'd seen on Evan's face had been for her.

For the remainder of the morning Jade stayed in her room and out of Evan's way. When she finished the piece she'd been working on for the magazine, she headed to the kitchen to grab something to eat.

She found Matthew seated at the kitchen table, a board game spread open in front of him.

"Hi, Matthew," Jade said.

"Hi," Matthew said, flashing a tentative smile.

"Where's Evan?" she asked, telling herself she simply wanted to know in order to continue to avoid him.

"He's clearing the snow off the sundeck," Matthew told her. "We're gonna play a game when he's done," he said as he picked the game pieces out of the box.

"That's nice," Jade said as she retrieved a block of cheddar cheese from the fridge. Cutting it into slices, she put them on a plate and located a box of crackers in the cupboard.

"Want to play checkers with me?" Matthew asked, gazing at her with a hopeful expression on his face.

Jade didn't have the heart to refuse. A quick game wouldn't hurt, she assured herself, as long as she was back upstairs before Evan reappeared.

"Sure," she said, and was instantly rewarded with a winning smile as she slipped into the chair opposite.

Matthew made the first move and the game was underway. Jade nibbled on the crackers and cheese as she played. One game quickly led to another and Jade soon forgot about wanting to avoid Evan.

Evan opened the door of the cabin and slipped quietly inside. Tugging off his father's boots, he set them on a mat nearby to dry before removing his down-filled jacket.

He'd just finished clearing snow from the sundeck and stairs during the brief lull in the storm, but the wind was rising again and a fresh layer of snow had started to fall.

The sound of Matthew's laughter echoing through the cabin brought a smile to Evan's lips, and not for the first time since he'd become guardian to the youngster, Evan marveled at the boy's resilience in the face of the tragedy of losing his parents.

Grief clutched at his heart anew when he remembered the two friends who'd had their lives snatched away in the blink of an eye.

But it had taken some time to adjust to the role of parent to a child he hardly knew. He'd been at a loss to know what to do or say to the boy who during those first pain-filled weeks had barely spoken three words to him.

Somehow he'd stumbled through. He'd taken two months' leave from his job because he felt Matthew needed the security of having someone around twenty-four hours a day.

A doctor friend of Evan's had suggested he encourage Matthew to talk about his parents to keep their memory alive. Though he'd been reluctant to heed the advice at first, the moment he'd tentatively brought up their names a look of relief had crossed Matthew's small features, and tears, the first Evan had seen, had pooled in the boy's eyes.

From that moment on, the change in Matthew had been remarkable. By talking about his parents, relating memories of times they'd shared, Evan had succeeded in opening a door for Matthew, allowing him to release his feelings of grief, feelings he'd kept bottled up inside.

As a result, a strong bond of love and trust had been forged between them and since then they'd never looked back. Evan had hired a live-in housekeeper and for a time their lives had settled into something of a pattern.

But a month ago his housekeeper had quit due to ill health, and finding a suitable replacement had become an impossible task.

Shortly after that, Evan had received a letter from a lawyer in San Francisco requesting his and Matthew's presence at a hearing granted to Matthew's aunt and uncle, Barbara and Alex Turner, who'd decided quite out of the blue to contest Evan's right to raise the boy.

The sound of renewed laughter broke through Evan's musings. With a sigh he pushed his problems aside for the moment and strode down the hall to the kitchen.

"Uh-oh, checkers," Evan said, seeing the board game spread out on the table. "Sorry, Jade. I should have warned you."

"Warned me about what?" Jade kept her gaze on

Matthew, ignoring the leap her pulse took in reaction to his appearance.

"When it comes to checkers, there's just no beating this kid." Evan ruffled the boy's hair in a gesture of affection before pouring himself a cup of coffee from the carafe on the counter.

"Sounds like you two get to play often," Jade commented, and at her words Matthew nodded vigorously, his smile wide.

Evan laughed and the sound sent a ripple of awareness down Jade's spine.

"Matthew doesn't go anywhere without his game of checkers," Evan explained. "How many times has he beaten you?"

Jade darted Evan a quick glance. "Five," she replied, refraining from adding that she'd been surprised at Matthew's speed and skill.

"I'm teaching him chess now," Evan went on. "My bet is it won't be long before he'll be a master at that, too," he added with more than a hint of pride.

"It's great you two can spend so much time together," Jade commented.

"Easy enough when we live in the same house," Evan said, pulling out a third chair. "Besides, Matthew's addicted," he continued with a grin. "He insists on playing a game each night before bed as well as hearing a bedtime story."

"Matthew lives with you...permanently?" Jade couldn't stop herself from asking.

"As his legal guardian that's part of the deal. Right, squirt?" Evan said, flashing the boy a grin.

"Right!" Matthew responded easily. "Can we

play a game of chess now?'' he asked. ''You said when you came in we could....'' he coaxed gently.

Evan's grin widened. ''Hank keeps a chess set in the living room,'' he said. ''You'll find it in a box on the bookshelf. Why don't you set it up in there? I'll be along when I've topped up my coffee.''

''Okay!'' Matthew hopped down from the chair and scurried from the room.

''Thanks for keeping an eye on him,'' Evan said as he rose and crossed to the counter.

Though Jade heard his words, her mind was still trying to digest the news concerning Matthew. ''I had no idea....'' she mumbled almost to herself.

''That I was Matthew's legal guardian, you mean?'' Evan quickly picked up on her train of thought.

''You never mentioned it,'' she said, meeting his eyes.

''Philip and Nina asked me shortly after Matthew was born,'' Evan explained. ''But I never expected I'd ever have to take on the responsibility.''

''No, I suppose not,'' Jade said, hearing the mixture of pain and sorrow in his voice. ''You appear to be managing very well. In fact I'd say you're doing a great job,'' she added, thinking it impossible not to admire Evan for accepting the responsibility of raising a child, a child who wasn't his own flesh and blood.

''So far, so good,'' Evan said, but Jade heard a hint of anxiety in his voice. Tempted as she was to pursue the subject, she bit back the question suddenly hovering on her lips.

Evan, who'd been staring off into the distance,

suddenly drew himself up. "Excuse me, I imagine Matthew's eager to start another chess lesson."

Jade sat for a long moment, her thoughts lingering on Evan and his role as Matthew's guardian. It was obvious from watching them together they'd formed a loving relationship, one as close as any real father and son. Jealousy stabbed at her and she quickly chastised herself for her weakness.

How could she be jealous of Matthew? He'd endured much more than any child should have to deal with. What was difficult to come to terms with however, was the fact Evan had obviously committed himself to the role of surrogate father but he'd been unable to commit himself to a relationship with her.

It was after the evening meal, a meal Jade had cooked, that she began to feel restless. After helping her clear away the dishes and tidy the kitchen, Evan and Matthew had wandered off to play another game of chess.

Jade told herself she was foolish to feel left out— Evan's devotion to Matthew was highly commendable. But she found herself dwelling on the notion of what might have been.

Annoyed at her own maudlin thoughts, she decided what she needed was a breath of fresh air. A short walk would help her sleep.

Though her boots weren't altogether suitable for trudging through deep snow, she felt reasonably confident if she kept to the path Evan and Matthew had shoveled on their foray outside, she could at least make it once around the perimeter of cabin.

Collecting her sheepskin coat from the closet,

Jade pulled on her knee-high boots and quietly let herself out. It had stopped snowing, and through the gaps in the clouds Jade could see some stars twinkling in the sky.

The air was cold and crisp and invigorating. The stark whiteness of the snow cast an eerie brightness as Jade made her way past her car and along the side of the cabin.

As she turned the corner the wind whipped her breath away and she gasped aloud as its icy fingers nipped at her cheeks and brought tears to her eyes.

Snowflakes were suddenly dancing around her, landing in her hair and on her eyelashes. She tucked her hair inside the collar of her jacket and fastened the top button before quickly thrusting her cold fingers into the warmth of her pockets.

The temperature was steadily dropping and the falling snowflakes had already begun to form a fresh white carpet on the newly cleared pathway.

Carefully picking her way along the side of the cabin, she rounded the second corner and came to a halt at the foot of the stairs leading to the sundeck. She stood for several minutes sheltered from the icy blast, staring across the wide expanse of frozen lake.

Jade found the silence infinitely soothing and she could feel the tension, caused no doubt by the presence of the man she'd once loved with all her youthful heart, slowly begin to dissipate.

Taking a deep cleansing breath, Jade shivered as she surveyed the Arctic-like scene. The freezing wind began to pick up and she snuggled deeper into the collar of her coat, wishing now she'd grabbed a hat from the closet.

At dinner Evan had commented that the weather report was predicting the storm would blow itself out by noon the following day. Road crews would possibly reach them later in the afternoon.

Jade's glance lingered on the ice-covered lake, glittering like one enormous diamond in the eerie light. She'd always believed there was something special about Paradise Lake, something magical, and suddenly she was glad she'd come.

With a sigh she turned and headed up the stairs to the sundeck. The stair risers were as slippery as a skating rink, and before she even had time to take her hands out of her pockets, her right foot slid from the third step, throwing her body off balance and pitching her backward.

Evan crossed to the liquor cabinet and poured himself a brandy. He carried the glass to the big bay window and stood staring out at the white landscape at a view that never failed to soothe him.

But not tonight. Because he was still no nearer a solution to the problem facing him. And time was running out.

Anger clenched like a fist inside him at the possibility of losing Matthew. During the past year the boy had come to mean everything to him.

Nina's sister and brother-in-law's sudden decision to challenge his right to raise Matthew had come as a complete surprise.

But the true reason behind their challenge had quickly become apparent. It had nothing to do with the welfare of the young boy and everything to do with the fact that Matthew would one day inherit a substantial amount of money from his deceased parents' estate.

Alex and Barbara Turner knew exactly what they were doing and why they were doing it. And to that end they had somehow garnered enough sympathy, pulled enough strings and been granted a hearing.

Evan had called a lawyer friend in San Francisco who was exploring various avenues of recourse, but he was growing increasingly discouraged by the fact his friend had been unable to have the hearing canceled.

The possibility of the judge ruling against Evan and in favor of the mercenary couple seemed improbable if not idiotic, but Evan couldn't quite bring himself to dismiss the threat, and the thought of losing Matthew was steadily eating away at him.

Disgust at the Turners' greed at the expense of a child brought a bitter taste to Evan's mouth and he downed the remainder of the brandy in an effort to wash it away.

Suddenly the eerie silence was broken by a thump and a muffled cry.

Evan frowned in puzzlement. Not burglars, surely. He dismissed the notion. Jade perhaps? Had she gone out?

Evan yanked on the sliding glass door leading to the sundeck. An icy blast met him, instantly stealing the breath from his lungs, but he ignored the biting wind and quickly crossed to the top of the stairs.

His heart leapt into his mouth when he saw Jade, lying like a limp rag doll, on the snow-covered ground below.

Chapter Four

Evan flew down the stairs two at a time, heedless of the slippery conditions. Jade's hair was spread out on the snow like a colorful copper scarf and her face looked as white as a sheet.

Heart pounding, Evan placed his fingertips at her throat. A wave of relief washed over him when he felt the steady beat of her pulse.

Jade moaned and attempted to lift her head.

"Lie still," Evan instructed. With quick, controlled movements he assured himself no bones were broken. But she did have a small bump on the back of her head. Gently, almost reverently, he brushed her hair off her forehead, and as he gazed down at her pale features, a forgotten emotion quivered briefly somewhere deep inside him.

Her eyelids fluttered open and he saw both confusion and pain in their depths.

"Let's get you inside," Evan said. Sliding one

hand under the collar of her jacket and the other beneath her knees, he tensed his muscles and smoothly lifted her off the frozen ground.

Her moan of pain and protest was lost as her head lolled against his shoulder. Tightening his grip he climbed the slippery steps to the sundeck. She felt like a featherweight in his arms and she made no protest as he carried her through the living room to his bedroom in the guest suite.

With infinite care Evan lowered Jade onto the bed, quickly removing her cumbersome sheepskin jacket. As he pulled off her leather boots he ground his teeth in annoyance when he saw that her boots were designed for looks and not for snowy weather conditions.

"What happened?" Jade mumbled, her eyes still shut.

"You fell," Evan replied. "Your jeans are wet. I'm taking them off," he informed her.

With the expertise of someone who has on numerous occasions removed clothes from a sleeping child, Evan unsnapped Jade's jeans and eased them over her hips, ignoring the quick jolt of his pulse at the sight of the small triangle of black lace covering her lower abdomen.

"My head...it hurts...." Jade muttered.

"I'm not surprised," Evan said. "Might as well take your sweater off, too," he went on. As he pulled her arms free, she moaned again. Her eyes opened but only for a moment.

Evan tugged the duvet cover over her, his gaze lingering for one brief second on the matching black lace bra she wore. He clenched his jaw and ignored his body's reaction to her near nakedness.

After tossing her sweater onto the nearby chair where he'd thrown her jeans, he studied her prone figure, quietly assessing the situation.

He guessed she'd slid on the icy stairs and cracked her head on the ice when she fell, but with the telephone out of order and snowy weather conditions, he had no way of getting her to a doctor.

Evan sat down on the bed and, leaning forward, brought his mouth to Jade's ear. He spoke softly but firmly. "Jade. Jade. Sweetheart, wake up."

"Mmm…" Jade responded, but her eyes remained closed.

Evan bent over her once more. "Come on, Jade, open your eyes," he coaxed.

This time her eyes flickered opened and she stared up at him, a rather bemused expression on her face. "Evan, you're back," she said, her mouth curving into a welcoming smile.

Jade tugged her hands free of the covers and reached up to touch his cheek. At the contact, a need he hadn't felt in a long time had Evan's stomach muscles tightening.

He quickly captured her hand, holding it against his cheek, and for a heart-aching moment he allowed himself the forgotten pleasure of pressing his lips to the sensitive chord at her wrist, enjoying her faint quiver of response.

"How do you feel?" Evan asked, clasping her hand gently in his.

Jade's eyes flickered open and this time she held his gaze. "My head hurts," she replied, grimacing a little. "Did I have too much wine at dinner?" Her eyelids drifted closed once more. "Kiss me, Evan," she pleaded softly. "Be my Prince Charming and wake me with a kiss..." Her words trailed off in a seductive whisper.

It was all Evan could do not to comply with her sleepy request and crush her mouth under his. Drawing a ragged breath, his lip curled into a twisted smile.

"Later," he said, but Jade had already drifted off to sleep.

From her comments it was obvious she was both confused and disoriented, believing it to be another time, another place. But she had recognized him and her pupils had appeared normal, at least to him.

Evan sat staring at Jade for several minutes before rising from the bed. Dragging a hand through his hair, he crossed to the window, his thoughts in a turmoil.

Behind him Jade slowly opened her eyes. She couldn't understand why she was lying in bed or why her head was pounding. Her gaze came to rest on Evan standing with his back to her at the window and she felt her heart kick against her rib cage in startled reaction.

Suddenly she realized that she wasn't in her own bed. She was in Evan's bed in the guest suite. How had she gotten there?

"Why am I here?" she asked, attempting to ease herself into a sitting position, only to fall back against the pillows as the pain in her head intensified.

Evan turned and quickly came toward her. "Don't

try to sit up," he cautioned. "You fell. Don't you remember?"

"Fell?" she repeated. "Oh...yes, I remember now. The stairs up to the deck were slippery," she said. "I think I must have hit my head on the ice."

"You did. You have a bump back there to prove it. But the skin isn't broken," Evan assured her.

Jade located the small swelling at the back of her head. "Ouch...I found it." She gently probed the area, managing a weak smile.

"Do you feel dizzy or nauseous?" Evan asked, moving closer.

"No." Jade tried to sit up again. She had to get out of there.

She thrust aside the duvet cover, only to grab it again and haul it up to her chin when she realized she was wearing only her underwear.

"I don't think you should get up, at least not yet," Evan advised.

"I'm fine, really," she insisted, determined to return to her own room, no matter what.

Ignoring the pain throbbing in her head, Jade shifted to the edge of the bed. She clutched the duvet cover tightly in one hand and stood up.

At once the carpet seemed to rush up to meet her, and she swayed like an aspen in a summer breeze.

Evan was at her side in an instant, his arm going around her to steady her. "What's your hurry?" he scolded gently. "You've had a nasty knock. You need to take it easy, at least for a little while." His breath fanned her forehead, sending her pulse skittering wildly.

Jade leaned against his rock-hard frame, glad of

his strength and support but not altogether sure if the weakness she was experiencing was a result of the bump she'd received or due to the fact she was in Evan's arms.

The tantalizing scent of his lime and leather aftershave was creating havoc with her senses, and the urge to drop her head onto his broad shoulder was almost more than she could resist.

"Let's get you back into bed," Evan said, and before she could protest he gently scooped her into his arms and deposited her on the bed.

At the unexpected action, Jade relaxed her grip on the duvet cover, letting it slip away to reveal her lacy black bra.

Evan calmly adjusted the duvet to cover her breasts and then withdrew. "That's not a blush I see, is it?" he teased, obviously glimpsing the rush of color invading her cheeks, a reaction she wished she could hide. "Why so modest, Jade?" he continued in the same tone. "There isn't an inch of you I haven't explored...intimately.... Or have you forgotten?"

Jade felt her breath catch in her throat. No, she hadn't forgotten, doubted she would ever forget the depth of passion he could incite with nothing more than a smoldering look or a fleeting caress.

Closing her eyes, she shut out Evan's unforgettable features. It wasn't enough that she felt as weak and vulnerable as a newborn baby, but lying practically naked in his bed was having a profound effect on her senses, evoking memories she'd just as soon keep locked away.

Tears stung her eyes and she squeezed her eyelids

tight in the faint hope of preventing them from escaping. But to her dismay she felt a wetness on her
cheek and angrily brushed it away.

"Get some sleep, Jade," Evan said softly. "I'd
carry you upstairs but there seems little point.
Oh...and don't worry, your virtue is safe with me.
I'll sleep on the couch in the living room." She
heard the trace of humor in his voice and wondered
at the prick of pain that stabbed her heart.

Jade waited until the door closed before she ventured to open her eyes and assure herself he had
truly gone. The knot of tension his remarks had
evoked gradually began to loosen, only to be replaced by a feeling of utter exhaustion. It had been
a year since she'd sparred verbally with Evan and
she was definitely out of practice.

With a sigh Jade closed her eyes and in a matter
of seconds sleep claimed her once again.

Jade woke with a start and stared at the shadows
in the room, knowing instinctively something was
different. Her head ached, and as she stretched, she
was aware that the muscles in her legs and back felt
stiff and sore.

All at once the events of the previous evening
came rushing back. And just to confirm it hadn't
been a dream, she gently probed her hair, easily lo-
cating the small bump on the back of her head.

The pain in her head had all but vanished, and as
she lay in the predawn darkness, she suddenly had
a vague recollection of hearing Evan's voice talking
to her, gently rousing her, several times throughout
the night.

Pushing the duvet cover aside, Jade swung her legs over the edge of the bed, relieved to discover there was no dizziness.

Her muscles ached a little as she crossed to the light switch near the door and flipped it on. A sound from the hallway sent her heart thundering in her breast and she scooped up her jeans and sweater, quickly pulling them on, fearful Evan might appear at any second.

Anxious to return to her own room and revitalize herself with a hot shower, Jade quietly let herself out of the guest bedroom.

She made her way down the hallway, praying silently that she wouldn't run into Evan. When she reached the living room she heard the deep, rich sound of Evan's voice raised in anger.

Frowning, Jade slowed her footsteps. Surely Evan wasn't shouting at Matthew? The door to the living room was ajar and, tiptoeing toward it, she put her ear to the opening.

"The phone lines were down yesterday—that's why you couldn't get through. And damn it, Kelly," Evan almost shouted, "I hired you to see if you could put a stop to the proceedings. Now you're telling me the date of the hearing's been changed and we have to be in San Francisco the day after tomorrow?"

Evan grabbed the base of the telephone from the end table and began to pace the room as far as the cord would allow.

"Matthew doesn't need this. I don't need this," he continued, exasperation in his tone. "How the

Turners ever managed to pull this off, I'll never know. Tell me again why I should even bother to show up?''

''Because you were the one who insisted they be kept informed of Matthew's progress,'' Kelly said. ''You thought that because they were his aunt and uncle and directly related to him, you should keep the doors of communication open. Appearing before the judge is an act of good faith on your part.''

''I just hate to have to put Matthew through this,'' he said.

''If you don't show up and deal with this threat now, then somewhere down the line it will come back to haunt you. Trust me,'' Kelly said.

''I do…and, you're right,'' Evan acknowledged. ''The only trouble is, I'm not sure we can be there on such short notice. I'm here at my father's cabin in Oregon and there's a snowstorm raging outside.''

''Well…being stranded in a snowstorm would certainly be considered a viable reason to ask for the meeting to be rescheduled. What's the forecast?'' Kelly asked.

''The storm is supposed to blow itself out by around noon today,'' Evan replied. ''But even if the forecast is right it's unlikely the road crews will get this far until tomorrow morning.''

''Just do your best. Hopefully the phone lines will stay open and you can keep me posted,'' Kelly said. ''But try to be here. The Turners are pulling out all the stops and, Evan, much as I hate to say this, they do appear to have built a case.''

''What the hell are you talking about?'' Evan

spun around, sending the phone cord whipping away and almost knocking over a plant.

"They're maintaining your job takes you away from Matthew too much," his lawyer stated calmly. "And they're arguing they can provide a more stable environment in which to raise the boy," she told him. "It's too bad you're housekeeper isn't still around. Have you found a replacement yet?"

"No," Evan said on a sigh. "So you're saying I already have two strikes against me?" He turned to stare out at the frozen lake, anger tightening like a fist inside him.

"I'm afraid that's how it looks at the moment," came the reply. "What you need is a wife," Kelly continued, her tone light and teasing. "I'd apply for the post myself but I don't think my fiancé would take too kindly to that." She chuckled softly.

Evan made no reply, his thoughts drifting for a moment to the woman asleep down the hall in his bed. An idea as simple as it was outrageous flashed into his mind.

"Sorry, what did you say?" Evan asked a moment later, realizing Kelly was speaking again.

"I said, don't be discouraged. We have a strong case, too. Try not to worry," Kelly went on.

"Thanks," Evan said. "I'll call if we can't make it, but weather permitting, we'll see you the day after tomorrow." Evan said. "Oh…and Kelly, I'm prepared to do anything—I repeat, *anything* to stop the Turners."

"Sounds like you have a plan in mind," Kelly ventured.

"I might. I'll get back to you." He jammed the receiver into its resting place.

Realizing Evan had hung up, Jade quickly withdrew and scurried up the stairs to her room. The little she'd been able to hear of Evan's conversation puzzled her. What had he meant when he'd said he had two strikes against him? And why did he have to be in San Francisco the day after tomorrow?

That he was angry had been obvious by his brusque tone but she couldn't fathom the reason for it, and besides, she reminded herself, it really wasn't any of her business.

Back in her bedroom Jade gathered a towel, another pair of jeans and a sweatshirt from the chest of drawers and slipped across the hall to the bathroom.

She stripped and stepped into the shower, where she carefully shampooed her hair. The hot spray pulsing on her back helped ease her aching muscles and, feeling a little more human, she dried herself off and returned to her bedroom.

Though the swelling had gone down, the area around it was still tender and so she sat on the bed and gently rubbed her wet hair between the folds of the towel.

The knock at her bedroom door sent her pulse into high gear. It was probably Matthew, she thought. Releasing the breath trapped in her lungs, she rose to open the door.

"Morning," Evan greeted her. "I came to see how you're feeling. I got worried when I couldn't find you. No aftereffects, I hope?"

Jade's heart jolted against her rib cage at the sight of him. He looked rather bedraggled, as if he'd spent the night in his clothes. He needed a shave and a shower, but as she preceded him into her room she was all too aware of the strong masculine scent that was his alone.

"A few aches and pains, that's all," she acknowledged. When her legs hit the bed she quickly sat down. "My head still hurts, but nothing I can't handle."

"Good," Evan said. "You should take things easy today," he suggested. "Stay inside."

"I plan to," she replied, silently adding that she also planned to avoid him as much as possible. The bedroom was small and she found his presence more than a little overwhelming. With nervous fingers she picked up the towel from the bed, gently rubbed her wet hair, all the while wishing he would leave.

But Evan stayed. "The storm appears to have run its course. The wind has eased up," he told her. "With any luck we'll be out of here tomorrow morning sometime."

"Great," Jade replied. She glanced up at him and was surprised at the tension she could see etched on his face. "Is Matthew awake yet?" she asked.

"Not yet." Evan turned and ran his hand across the back of his neck. That he had something on his mind was obvious, but Jade resolutely reminded herself it wasn't any of her business. She didn't want to know....

"Jade." Her name on his lips stilled her hands and sent a quiver of response chasing up her spine but she forced herself to ignore it as she raised her eyes to meet his.

The expression of despair she could see in the depths of his blue eyes spoke volumes. "What's wrong, Evan?" she asked, forgetting her resolve not to question him. "Is Hank..." Fear for the older man had her rising to her feet.

"Hank's fine," Evan assured her, then hesitated.

Jade sank down on the bed again. "*Something's* wrong," she said.

Evan sighed. "That's one way to describe it, I suppose," he answered cryptically. She watched as he inhaled deeply before continuing. "I need to ask you a favor, a rather big favor," he said at last.

"What kind of a favor?" she asked cautiously.

"It's really for Matthew," Evan said, and Jade watched in fascination as Evan raked both hands through his dark silky hair before spinning away, muttering under his breath.

Something was definitely wrong. She'd never seen Evan behave like this before. "If I can help Matthew in any way, I will," she said, sincerity echoing through her voice.

In the short time she'd known Matthew she'd come to like and admire the young boy both for his intelligence and charm as well as for his strength and emotional resilience in face of the loss he'd suffered.

"I need a wife," Evan said.

Jade was sure she was dreaming, sure that the knock on the head she'd received the night before had somehow affected her hearing.

"A wife?" she repeated, staring at Evan as if he'd suddenly sprouted a pair of antlers.

"Yes, a wife," he confirmed.

"But...I mean...I don't understand," Jade stammered, glad she was already sitting down because his words had had the impact of a speeding train.

"Let me explain," Evan was quick to jump in. "I told you I became Matthew's guardian when Philip and Nina were killed in the plane crash," he began. "Being thrust into the role of parent to a young child I'd seen only a couple of times when he was a baby was daunting, to say the least. But I'd made a promise to my friends—" He broke off and turned away, starting to pace.

"I won't bore you with all the details," he went on after a brief pause. "Suffice it to say, both Matthew and I had to make adjustments. But we got through. Together...we made it. He's a great kid—" Evan ground to a halt once more.

"Now the Turners, Matthew's aunt and uncle, have decided to challenge my guardianship. They're arguing that my job takes me away from Matthew too much, that he isn't being properly taken care of...." His disgust was evident in his tone.

"They're also saying they can offer a better...family environment." He shook his head. "Somehow they've convinced a judge in San Francisco—that's where they live—to agree to a hearing.

"These are the same people who never bothered to visit Matthew after the funeral, the same people who didn't even send him a birthday or Christmas card. The same people who haven't at any time during the past year picked up the phone to even talk to Matthew.'' Evan stopped pacing and came to a halt in front of the window. Jade could almost see the anger coming off him in waves.

"Surely in view of what you've told me about the Turners, they don't have a chance of getting custody of Matthew?'' Jade ventured.

Evan spun around to face her. "Courts can be tricky. I've heard all sorts of horror stories involving custody cases. And there is the fact that they are related by blood. Who knows what a judge might do?'' he replied. "Matthew means everything to me,'' he went on, and at his words Jade felt a hand squeeze her heart.

"The truth is the Turners have a personal agenda, one that has nothing to do with Matthew's welfare or his feelings.'' He stopped and drew a ragged breath before continuing. "The only reason they're trying to stir things up is because they've found out Matthew will inherit a tidy sum when he's older. No doubt their plan includes getting their greedy hands on it.''

"But surely that money's being held in trust for Matthew?'' Jade asked.

"Of course,'' Evan replied, coming to a halt in front of her. "But trusts can and have been broken. That's why I've come up with a plan to make damned sure their scheme never gets off the ground.''

"A plan?'' Jade repeated, slowly beginning to realize exactly where he was heading.

Evan dropped to a crouch in front of her and took both her hands in his. A frisson of excitement and alarm shot up her arms.

It took every ounce of strength she possessed to meet his gaze.

"If I were to arrive at the hearing with…my wife, the Turners' case would be blown out of the water," he said evenly.

Jade blinked and swallowed the hard lump of emotion clogging her throat.

His eyes seemed to bore into hers, willing her to say yes. And for a mesmerizing moment Jade was sorely tempted to nod her consent. Sanity prevailed and she dropped her gaze, breaking the spell.

She inhaled a ragged breath. "I really don't think—" she began, then stopped abruptly when she saw a flash of anger and frustration in his eyes, along with another emotion, one he quickly controlled.

Evan's sigh was heartfelt. "Jade, I know this is a lot to ask. But I made a promise to Nina and Philip and to Matthew, a promise I intend to keep. Matthew's been through enough heartache. Please, won't you think about it—for his sake?" Evan urged, his eyes revealing none of the emotions she'd glimpsed only a moment ago.

His passionate plea together with his nearness and the emotional intensity of the situation was affecting her deeply, and it was becoming increasingly difficult for her to think clearly.

"I don't—" she began.

"I'm not asking for a permanent arrangement. Six months to a year at the most," he cut in. "Please. Just think about it," he repeated, his gaze riveted to hers.

Jade's resolve collapsed like a house of cards.

"All right, I'll think about it," she relented, and instantly saw the flash of relief that appeared in his eyes.

"Thank you," Evan said, giving her hand a gentle squeeze. "I'd better check on Matthew," he added, and with a fleeting smile he rose and left the room.

Jade sat for a long moment while the conversation replayed inside her head. She'd heard the barely suppressed rage in Evan's voice when he'd spoken of the Turners; she'd seen the anger in every line of his body. She knew Evan was deeply committed to Matthew.

A profound sadness washed over her when she thought of what might have been. From the moment he'd proposed to her that hot summer night over a year ago, she'd begun weaving dreams of having a family. She'd imagined herself in the role of a stay-at-home mother, caring and nurturing their children while Evan flew around the countryside in search of the best news stories.

Her dream had been shattered by their breakup and been made all the more emotionally devastating when she'd lost their child. There was a certain irony in the fact that Evan had asked her to be his wife simply to retain custody of a child he hadn't fathered.

Chapter Five

He needed a wife! A bubble of hysterical laughter threatened to burst forth and Jade quickly clamped a hand over her mouth. Rising from the bed, she crossed to the window, blinking rapidly to stop the tears gathering behind her eyes.

Keeping her gaze focused on the snow-covered countryside, she took several deep, steadying breaths, drawing some small measure of comfort from the peaceful scene outside.

Gradually the threat of tears diminished and the ache in her heart subsided, but the pain throbbing inside her head remained.

Evan's proposal, if what he'd said could even be construed as one, had been a far cry from the one he'd issued on a hot August night sixteen months ago....

"Marry me!" He'd spoken the words in a husky

whisper less than eight hours after she'd arrived at
the cabin.

They'd been standing side by side on the sundeck
gazing out across the water, watching the sun paint
a silver ribbon of light on the lake as it made its
slow descent toward the horizon.

Her heart had leapt into her throat, and she'd
thrown him a startled glance, trying to decide if he'd
actually spoken or if her imagination had simply
been playing tricks on her.

He'd met her gaze and his handsome features had
creased into a smile so devastating, it had instantly
ignited a spark of desire that spread like wildfire
through her body.

"Wha..? What did you say?" she'd asked, her
voice little more than a hoarse whisper.

Evan turned to face her. "You aren't dreaming,
Jade."

She had to swallow to alleviate the sudden dryness in her throat. "But I—"

Evan brought a finger to her lips. "I haven't even
kissed you? Is that what you were going to say?"
His tone was laced with amusement.

Totally mesmerized by the seductive quality of
his voice, Jade felt her heart shudder to a halt and
her breath lock in her throat.

"I intend to remedy that," he went on, gently
brushing his thumb back and forth against her lower
lip in a touch that was as exciting as it was erotic.

Jade gasped as the contact sent tiny electric cur-
rents of sensation spiraling through her, stirring to
life new and utterly unfamiliar flutterings low in her
abdomen.

''You are so beautiful....'' Evan told her before bringing his mouth to within a hairbreadth of her own. ''From the moment you arrived this afternoon I've been aching to do this,'' he said a split second before his mouth covered hers.

Desire, hot and incredibly arousing, sprinted through her with the speed and ferocity of a tornado, wreaking havoc along its path and leaving a trail of need that left her breathless and exhilarated and more alive than she'd ever felt in her life.

She couldn't seem to get enough of the dark exotic taste of him, a taste that sparked a response from somewhere deep inside, a response she hadn't known she was capable of feeling, a response that had her quivering with a need she'd only ever read about in the pages of romance novels.

But this was real—astonishingly, amazingly real—and as his tongue plundered the inner softness of her mouth in a dance of urgent invitation, she suddenly understood, for the first time in her twenty-two years of life, what the hoopla was all about.

So this was passion, this wild excitement vibrating through her, playing havoc with her senses and shattering her control.

With one mind-blowing kiss, one incredibly erotic melding of mouths, Evan had given her a taste of heaven, successfully obliterating from her memory the dozen or more meaningless kisses she'd received from other men she'd dated.

Her answer, when they'd finally come up for air, had been a breathless and emphatic ''Yes, I'll marry you.'' She'd believed in her heart she'd found the man of her dreams.

But four months later, in a hotel in New Orleans, her dream had dissolved with Evan's sudden and startling announcement that he'd changed his mind.

He'd told her coldly and bluntly that he'd made a mistake, that he wasn't willing to relinquish the freedom he'd enjoyed for so long, nor was he ready for the kind of commitment she wanted from him.

Although she'd sensed for several days something was troubling him, she'd assumed it had to do with the story he was working on and not their relationship.

He'd broken her heart, torn it to pieces with a few choice words and phrases, and Jade had resolved never again to throw herself with such foolish abandonment, such childish naiveté, into the arms of any man....

Not that he'd asked her to, she quickly reminded herself now. Evan's need for a wife was simply a means to an end, an expedient way to enable him to keep the promises he'd made to his friends Philip and Nina and, of course, to Matthew.

But while Jade understood and applauded his motives, she couldn't agree to what would essentially be nothing more than a marriage of convenience. Convenient for Evan, but potentially disastrous for her.

A marriage of convenience. The concept was old-fashioned and outdated, and Jade doubted anyone would be foolhardy enough to enter into such an arrangement.

Resolutely Jade reminded herself that she wasn't responsible for Evan's or Matthew's happiness, but as she made her way downstairs, a little voice inside her head, a voice she couldn't ignore, kept telling her Matthew would be devastated if he lost Evan.

In the kitchen Jade found Matthew in his pajamas seated at the table, a bowl of cereal in front of him.

"Good morning, Matthew," Jade greeted him with a smile and, crossing to the fridge, proceeded to pour herself a small glass of orange juice.

"Hi, Jade," Matthew responded.

"Where's Evan?" she asked before taking a sip of juice.

"In the shower," Matthew replied.

"Oh…" Jade's grip on the glass tightened and she felt her pulse pick up speed as an image of Evan standing naked in the shower flashed into her mind.

Annoyed at her reaction, she downed the remainder of the juice, then rinsed the empty glass. When the phone on the counter beside her rang she reached for the receiver.

"Hello!"

"Jade! So that's where you've been hiding," her godfather, Hank Mathieson, scolded, a note of relief in his voice. "I was beginning to worry," he added.

"*You* were beginning to worry!" Jade responded in an exasperated tone. "Now there's a switch. If anyone has been hiding it's you," she countered. "I called you three times on Friday and got no answer. I even called a couple of your cronies down in Paradise, but they said they hadn't seen neither hide nor hair of you for days."

"Jade, darlin', don't tell me you drove all the way to the cabin in that old jalopy of yours in the middle of a snowstorm just to check on me?" Hank said.

"What do you mean, old jalopy?" Jade responded. "I'll have you know I had my car serviced a month ago," she told him.

"Did you have snow tires put on?" Hank asked.

"No...but that's not the point—"

"Not the point!" Hank swore softly and succinctly in Jade's ear. "Jade Patricia Adams, you'll be the death of me yet," he ended on a sigh.

Jade chuckled. This kind of exchange was typical of their relationship and Jade wasn't sure who enjoyed the teasing banter more. "That's rich," she retorted, her laughter taking the edge off the words. "If I hadn't been worried about you I wouldn't have had to drive here in the first place. I was lucky to make it—" she broke off abruptly, realizing she'd just damned herself.

"Take your foot out of your mouth, darlin' girl, and tell me this, did Evan and Matthew make it to the cabin, too?" Hank's voice rumbled over the wires.

"Yes," Jade confirmed, and as if to verify her answer, Evan appeared in the kitchen doorway looking incredibly handsome, his hair still damp from the shower. "In fact, he's right here," she added, moved by the sight of him. She thrust the phone at Evan. "It's your father. He wants to talk to you."

"Oh...thanks." Evan's fingers lightly skimmed hers as he took the receiver from her, and at the contact, a shiver of awareness scurried up her arm.

Jade spun away, distressed by her body's unguarded reaction, and she would have left the kitchen, but when her glance flicked over to Matthew sitting at the table, she noticed with a twinge of concern that he looked ill.

Jade quickly crossed to the table. "Matthew? Are you all right?"

"I don't feel so good," Matthew said, his eyes filling with tears. "I think I'm going to be sick," he announced.

"Quick! Into the bathroom." Jade ushered Matthew from the kitchen and into the small adjacent bathroom.

Matthew barely made it in time. Jade stood beside him, an arm around his shoulders, her hand on his forehead, murmuring words of comfort as he threw up into the toilet bowl.

When he was done, Jade dampened a washcloth and gently wiped his pale face.

"Do you feel better now?" she asked, brushing a strand of hair off his damp forehead.

Matthew nodded.

"What's wrong? What happened?" The question came from Evan, who'd appeared in the open doorway.

With a heart-wrenching sob, Matthew ran toward Evan, who easily caught the boy and scooped him into his arms.

"He threw up," Jade told him. "He probably ate something that didn't agree with him," she added, offering the most obvious explanation.

"Hey, sport. It's all right," Evan said soothingly, but the boy buried his head in Evan's shoulder and continued to cry.

"Maybe you should go back to bed for a little while," Evan suggested.

Matthew sniffed and nodded, then pulled away to wipe his nose on the sleeve of his pajamas.

"Ca...ca...can Jade c-come and tuck me in?" He hiccuped.

Blue eyes swimming with unshed tears gazed pleadingly at Jade.

"Of course, I'll tuck you in," she said with a smile.

Evan made no response. Turning, he led the way down the hall to the guest suite.

In the second bedroom, Evan lowered Matthew to the floor and then moved aside to allow Jade to pass.

"Would you like a drink of water or juice?" Evan asked as Matthew climbed into bed.

"Water please," Matthew responded as Jade fluffed his pillows.

"I'll get it," she offered, but Evan quickly intervened.

"No...stay with him," he said. "I'll be right back," he added, flashing a brief smile before heading for the door.

As Jade smoothed the covers and tucked them in, she noticed several books sitting on the bedside table, along with Matthew's checker game.

"Ah...*The Wizard of Oz*." She picked up the book sitting on top. "This was one of my favorites when I was your age. My father read it to me almost every night." She smiled as she opened the pages and leafed through it.

"I like the Scarecrow best," Matthew told her.

"Me, too," Jade said. "Would you like me to read to you?" she asked, looking around for a chair.

"Okay," Matthew's expression brightened a little. "Evan always sits on the bed beside me," he told her. "You can, too, if you like." He slid over to make room for her on the single bed.

Jade hesitated, but seeing the hopeful look in Matthew's blue eyes, she didn't have the heart to refuse his invitation.

When Evan returned to the bedroom a few minutes later, he came to a halt in the doorway. Seeing Jade sitting on the bed with Matthew snuggled against her caused his heart to stumble inside his chest.

They looked so natural together. Matthew was leaning against Jade, his head pressed against her breast. The expression on Matthew's face as he gazed up at Jade was one of total trust, mixed with a strong dose of adoration.

He knew Matthew still felt the loss of his mother acutely, and while Mrs. Johanson, their housekeeper, had done in a pinch, it was obvious Matthew still needed—indeed, *longed for*—a mother's love.

Matthew had obviously taken a shine to Jade. And who could blame him? Evan thought. He'd had a similar reaction the first time he'd set eyes on her that hot August afternoon more than a year ago.

In truth he'd been totally bowled over by her genuine warmth and loving nature, her bright smile and wide-eyed innocence. But what had touched him much more profoundly had been the look of vulnerability he'd seen in her eyes.

He'd wanted to be her friend, her lover, her protector all rolled into one, and for the first time in his life he'd acted impulsively and emotionally. He'd asked her to marry him, and when she'd said yes, nothing before or since had seemed so right.

Jade had been the one who'd decided she should travel with him on his next assignment, and though he'd advised her to finish her degree first, she'd insisted, and wanting her by his side he hadn't tried too hard to dissuade her.

But during the four months of their engagement as they'd hopped from one city to the next, from one sleazy hotel room to the next while he'd pursued a story, he'd watched their relationship slowly unravel.

With the rather vagabond existence they were living and with few outside interests of her own to fill her free time, Jade had focused all her attention on him, wanting to know where he was going and when she could expect him to return.

She grew increasingly bored and restless, and because he was gone most of the day, there was little he could do to alleviate the situation. And Evan knew it was only a matter of time before Jade would start to resent him and the time he spent away from her.

After several weeks of soul-searching, he'd known he had to let her go, had to set her free to find herself.

Breaking their engagement had been the hardest thing he'd ever had to do. And though he'd known his actions had been both cruel and unfeeling, he'd thought a clean break was the simplest and best solution, at least for Jade.

He could still recall with vivid clarity the look of raw pain he'd seen in her eyes when he'd told her he wanted to postpone their wedding indefinitely.

But while he wasn't proud of what he'd done, his only regret was having to let her go.

Jade heard a soft sigh of sound and glanced up to see Evan standing in the doorway staring at her. For a fleeting moment she thought she glimpsed a look of longing in his eyes before his expression swiftly changed, almost as if shutters had been pulled down.

"Is something wrong?" she asked.

"No," Evan assured her as he moved toward the bed. "I just didn't want to interrupt," he explained easily.

"Jade's reading me *The Wizard of Oz,*" Matthew told him unnecessarily.

"I see that." Evan handed Matthew the glass of water. "Feeling better?" he asked.

"A little," Matthew replied.

"Maybe you should take a nap," Evan suggested once again as he placed his hand on the boy's forehead.

"But I'm not tired," Matthew insisted in a tone that bordered on petulant.

"Want me to read a little more?" Jade quickly intervened, wanting to distract Matthew.

"Yes, please," Matthew said, giving Jade a warm smile.

"I'll read one more chapter," she said. "Then you can have a nap."

"Okay," Matthew agreed without any argument.

"I'll go and make a few phone calls and find out if the road crews are out yet," Evan said. "I'll check back with you in a little while."

Evan withdrew once more and Jade continued to read, but after a few minutes she sensed a change

in Matthew and, glancing down at him, smiled when
she saw he'd fallen asleep.

Jade quietly closed the book and returned it to the
bedside table before gently easing herself off the
bed. As she arranged the covers around Matthew's
sleeping figure, a thought flashed into her mind. She
wondered if the reason Matthew had been ill was
because he knew of the Turners' bid to wrest him
away from Evan.

Anyone could see the relationship Matthew and
Evan shared was very special, and it was unthinkable that the Turners would deliberately put a child
through an emotional wringer for their own mercenary reasons.

Jade leaned over to drop a light kiss on Matthew's
cheek, silently reminding herself that this wasn't her
fight, that she'd be a fool to get involved.

When Jade entered the living room a few moments later, she found Evan sitting in his father's
chair, elbows on his knees, head in his hands, looking as if he had the whole world on his shoulders.

His head jerked up, and as their eyes met for a
brief moment, Jade glimpsed his look of utter despair. ''Is Matthew all right?'' he asked, rising.

''He's fine. He fell asleep,'' she told him, and
noted the relief that crossed his features.

''A nap will do him good,'' Evan said.

''He'll probably be as right as rain when he wakes
up,'' Jade added, wanting to reassure him.

Evan flashed her a grateful smile. ''I don't know
if I'm cut out to be a parent,'' he said with a sigh.
''There's a hell of a lot more to it than I ever realized.''

"You love him very much," Jade said, her words a statement of fact, not a question.

Evan's eyes locked on hers. "Yes," he replied, and Jade heard the catch in his voice. "That's why just the thought of losing him—" He broke off. He raked a hand through his hair and strode toward the window. "I can't lose him. I simply refuse to let it happen."

Jade heard the note of desperation in Evan's voice and understood the turmoil he was going through, having experienced firsthand the emotional pain of losing a child.

A feeling of sadness enveloped her and she spoke without thinking. "Sometimes there's nothing anyone can do." Her words were a mere whisper of sound, but the moment they were out, Jade wished them unsaid.

She darted a guilty glance at Evan's broad back, silently praying he hadn't heard her. Her prayer was answered.

"Sorry," Evan said as he turned to face her. "What did you say?" he asked, his tone casual.

Jade almost sagged with relief. "Nothing. It doesn't matter," she assured him. "I've been thinking about what you said earlier, about needing a wife," she continued, changing the subject to one she knew would distract him.

"And?" His eyes flashed to hers.

Jade swallowed convulsively. "I was wondering...well, I just thought... Couldn't you just say we're engaged to be married?" She blurted out the suggestion, not sure when she'd changed her mind about getting involved.

Evan held her gaze for several long seconds, his expression unreadable. ''Saying we're engaged won't be enough. Engagements can easily be broken, remember?''

There was no mistaking the irony in his voice, but behind it there was something else, a carefully concealed emotion—was it pain?

But before she could respond Evan spoke again.

''Look, Jade, I know after all that's happened between us I'm asking a lot.... But don't you see? If I introduce you as my wife it will seriously undermine the Turners' case, and with any luck the judge will throw out this new application of theirs to try to gain custody of Matthew.''

''But are you sure it will work?'' Jade asked, and felt her heart flutter when Evan brought his hands up to grasp her shoulders.

''Right now I'm not sure of anything,'' he told her in a heavy voice. ''All I know is I have to do something. Will you help me?''

Chapter Six

Jade felt her heart leap into her throat as Evan's eyes bored into hers, almost as if he were trying to see inside her soul. Beneath his hands a familiar heat began to radiate through her, arousing forgotten sensations, forbidden needs.

"Yes, I'll marry you," Jade said, and as she spoke, a feeling of déjà vu washed over her. She'd used the same words when she'd accepted Evan's first proposal, but this time there was none of the heady excitement racing through her, none of the intense joy, and there would be no dizzying kiss to seal the pledge they'd made to each other.

"Thank you," Evan said, his voice a husky whisper. "You won't regret this, I promise."

Before she had time to react, his mouth swooped down to claim hers.

Desire, hot and heavy, slammed into her, catapulting her at breakneck speed to the edge of control. Weak with a longing only he could arouse, she stumbled against him in the faint hope the contact would somehow appease the need steadily spreading to every nerve, every cell.

But the tantalizing feel of his body pressed firmly against hers only served to increase her frustration, and she moaned deep in her throat as wave upon wave of sensation washed over her, igniting a hunger only his total possession could assuage.

A trip to paradise was hers for the asking. She knew it by the familiar urgency of his kisses, the escalating sexual tension between them and the unmistakable evidence of his physical arousal nudging insistently at her abdomen.

Evan threaded his fingers through the silky softness of Jade's hair and felt his body tremble as her mouth softened in surrender. He tasted again the exotic sweetness that was hers alone and wondered vaguely how he'd managed to survive this long without her.

The scent of lavender and lilacs filled his head and swamped his senses. He couldn't seem to get enough of her, and when he heard her low rumble of frustration, a need he'd taught himself to forget tore at his insides, leaving him clinging with slippery fingers to what was left of his control.

Suddenly, like a brief summer squall, it was over and Evan found himself standing an arm's length away from Jade, feeling as if his heart had been torn from his body.

"No…!" Jade brought her hands up to prevent Evan from reaching for her again. On legs that were trembling, she retreated several steps, fighting to regain control of emotions gone dangerously awry.

"Jade, I'm sorry—" Evan began.

"Don't!" Jade quickly cut him off, surprised that her voice sounded steady when inside she was shaking like a leaf. "That should never have happened."

Color darkened Evan's cheeks and a muscle throbbed at his jaw. "Why not?" he challenged. "I rather enjoyed it, and I got the distinct impression you did, too."

"Fishing for compliments, Evan?" Jade countered, feeling the need to erect some kind of barrier between them. "That's not like you," she added, struggling to douse the fire he'd lit within her.

She was still reeling from the kiss, a kiss that proved she wasn't as immune to him as she'd believed. He'd seduced her with mind-blowing kisses once before, only to toss her aside when he'd grown tired of her, and she knew she'd be a fool to give him a chance to break her heart a second time.

"I just sealed our bargain the conventional way," Evan told her, his tone casual. "Isn't that what newly engaged couples do? Or are you already having second thoughts?"

There was something in his voice that made her glance up at him, and for a fleeting second an emotion she couldn't decipher flickered in the depths of his eyes.

"No," Jade replied with a calmness she was far from feeling. "But I do have one condition," she went on, surprising herself with her words. The idea had just popped into her head, and like a drowning man being thrown a life raft she grabbed it with both hands.

Evan threw her a startled look. "I'm listening," he said.

"The condition is that our marriage will be a marriage in name only—a marriage of convenience," she told him quickly before her courage failed her.

As she waited for Evan to respond, Jade could hear her heart hammering wildly as if it were trying to escape.

"If that's the way you want it, then I agree to your…condition," he said with icy formality, his expression controlled. "Now, if you have no objections, I'm going to call my lawyer and start the ball rolling," he added matter-of-factly.

"Fine," Jade replied, struggling to appear unaffected and trying hard to ignore the disappointment tugging at her. *Fool!* she derided herself. Surely she hadn't expected Evan to argue about the condition and insist their marriage be a real one?

"When do you have to be in San Francisco for the hearing?" Jade asked.

"It's scheduled for three o'clock tomorrow afternoon," he told her. "It's cutting things a bit fine, but the road crews are already clearing the main roads, and with luck we'll be able to leave early in the morning," he said. "I'll call the airlines and make reservations," he added as he reached for the telephone.

Turning his back on her, Evan began to dial and silently Jade withdrew, closing the door behind her. Out in the hallway she stood for several minutes wondering if she hadn't just made the biggest mistake of her life.

"Jade?"

The sound of Matthew's voice jolted her out of her reverie and she glanced down the hall to see him standing in the doorway, dressed in his jeans and a sweater.

"You're up and dressed! Feeling better?" Jade asked as he made his way toward her.

Matthew nodded. "I'm thirsty," he said.

"We can fix that," Jade responded. "Would you like apple juice, orange juice or water?"

"Apple juice, please," Matthew replied. "And can I have a piece of toast, too?"

"I don't see why not," she said, relieved he appeared to have recovered from his earlier upset.

"Where's Evan?" Matthew asked as he climbed onto the kitchen chair he'd vacated less than an hour ago.

"He's in the living room making some phone calls," Jade told him.

"Oh... Want to play a game of checkers with me?" Matthew asked, flashing a cheeky grin.

"Only if you let me win," she replied.

"Okay," Matthew replied, his tone serious.

"Thanks very much," Jade responded with a laugh as she ruffled his hair.

For the remainder of the morning Matthew kept Jade company in the kitchen. True to his promise he let Jade win a game, but hard as she tried to win a second, Matthew somehow managed to outsmart her.

Jade was busy making tuna sandwiches to accompany the tomato soup already warming on the stove when Evan appeared.

"Hey, sport. You're up. How are you feeling?" he greeted Matthew.

At the sound of Evan's voice, Jade jumped. How could she go through with this? How could she have proposed a marriage of convenience when just hearing his voice could set her heart to pounding?

"Okay, I guess," Matthew replied as he reset the pieces on the checkerboard. "Wanna play?"

"Sure," Evan responded.

"Who were you talking to on the phone?" Matthew wanted to know.

Evan finished pouring himself a cup of coffee. "First I spoke to Kelly. Then I had to call the airlines and get seats on a plane to San Francisco. We have to be there tomorrow to talk to the judge, remember?" Evan pulled out the chair next to Matthew and sat down.

Matthew groaned. "Do we have to?" he asked, his tone disrespectful. "I want to stay here."

"I'm afraid we can't." Evan bit back a sigh. Before leaving Boston he'd talked to Matthew about the Turners and the reason for their trip. He tried to be matter-of-fact, but he wondered if Matthew had picked up on the feelings of anger and frustration he'd been harboring throughout the past week.

"I don't want to see a stupid judge." Matthew slammed his hands down on the checkerboard, sending the pieces flying. "I want to stay here with you and Jade," he announced sulkily.

Jade spun around in time to see Matthew's blue eyes fill with tears, but before she could make a move toward him, Evan was on his feet, lifting the fractious boy into his arms.

"Hey, buddy, don't cry." Evan's tone was gentle as he patted Matthew's back. Over the boy's shoulder his gaze met Jade's and a dark eyebrow rose in what was unmistakably a question.

Jade knew he was asking her permission to tell Matthew their plan, and with only the briefest of hesitations she nodded.

"Matthew." Evan spoke softly into the boy's ear. "Jade and I have something important we want to tell you." At his words Matthew sniffed loudly and slowly pulled away to look at Evan.

"Wh-what?" Matthew asked.

"Let's sit down and I'll explain." Evan lowered himself onto the chair Matthew had vacated, balancing the child on his right knee.

Jade took the chair opposite, noting as she did the rather anxious look on Matthew's face. Her pulse picked up speed as she gave Matthew a smile, all the while wondering what his reaction would be to the news Evan was about to impart.

"What would you say if I told you Jade and I are going to get married?" Evan asked.

Matthew darted a look of wide-eyed surprise at Jade before shifting his gaze back to Evan. "Married?" he repeated. "You mean Jade would come and live with you and me all the time?"

"Yes," Evan replied, a hint of a smile tugging at the corners of his mouth.

"And we'd be a real family? Like when I had my mom and dad?" Matthew wanted to know, obviously trying to sort the situation out in his head.

Jade caught the look of sorrow that flashed across Evan's face and silently she fought her own battle for control, blinking back the tears stinging her eyes.

"Something like that," she heard Evan say in a gruff voice.

Matthew gazed intently at Evan, as if he couldn't quite take it all in, as if he was afraid to believe. "Cross your heart?" Matthew asked.

"Cross my heart," Evan echoed the phrase and, using his free hand, made the familiar motion against his heart. Seconds later Matthew threw his arms around Evan.

Over Matthew's shoulder Evan's gaze collided with Jade's and for a breathless moment she felt her heart trip at the look of love she could see shining in their depths.

It was for Matthew, of course, Jade hurriedly reminded herself as she tried unsuccessfully to ignore the hopeless longing tugging at her.

Matthew released his hold on Evan and, sliding to the floor, he turned to shyly look at Jade.

Jade swallowed the lump of emotion lodged in her throat. "Matthew, I know we've only known each other such a short time," she began tentatively, not sure just what to say. "But I like you a lot and I'd be proud to be your friend."

"I like you, too," Matthew responded softly. "And I'm glad you're going to be my new mom," he added in a rush before launching himself at her.

As Jade gathered Matthew into her arms, it was all she could do to hold back the tears pooling in her eyes. She held him tight while her throat burned with emotion at his loving display.

Jade was careful to avoid Evan's gaze, fearful of what he might see in her eyes. For Matthew to accept her so readily had everything to do with how much he loved and trusted Evan.

The doubts she'd been harboring regarding her agreement to participate in Evan's plan to stop the Turners dissipated like dust in the wind, leaving behind another emotion, one she wasn't altogether sure she should analyze.

Lunch was a relatively quiet affair. Matthew's excited chatter filled the tense silences. That he was thrilled with Evan's news was patently obvious by his constant smile and his reluctance to leave Jade's side.

Much as she was curious to know what arrangements Evan had made with respect to their upcoming marriage, it wasn't until after they'd tucked a tired but happy Matthew into bed that the opportunity to discuss the subject finally presented itself.

"Jade, before you rush off, I thought you might like to know the plan of action for tomorrow," Evan said as they left Matthew's room.

"Fine," Jade replied. "Thanks," she added as he held open the door to the living room.

Evan followed her in and crossed to the liquor cabinet. "I'm having a brandy. Will you join me?" he asked over his shoulder.

Jade came to a halt at the window. "No, thank you," she responded, thinking that Evan's presence was intoxicating enough.

"Tomorrow's going to be a long day. We have

quite a bit of ground to travel,'' he said as, glass in hand, he came to stand beside her.

"The storm has blown itself out and it's fortunate the road crews made it this far,'' Jade said.

They'd heard the heavy vehicles earlier that afternoon and Evan had flagged one down and talked to two of the workmen.

"The driver of the snowplow suggested taking Route 62 South to Medford. He said it had been cleared and sanded and was in pretty good shape.'' Evan swirled the contents of his glass before taking a sip. "We're booked on the eleven o'clock flight to Reno,'' he went on, "then on the one o'clock flight from Reno to 'Frisco.''

"Reno?'' Jade threw a questioning glance at Evan.

"That's right,'' Evan confirmed. "I've already called and made arrangements for us to get married at a chapel not far from the airport,'' he told her.

"But I thought—''

"Unfortunately we don't have the luxury of spending weeks or months to plan this wedding,'' Evan cut in. "A side trip to Reno eliminates the necessity for blood tests and the normal three-day waiting period required by most states.''

"I see,'' Jade responded, surprised at the impatient tone in his voice.

"Next, you'll be telling me you don't have anything suitable to wear for a wedding,'' he hurried on.

Jade bristled at the implication behind his words. "I certainly don't need any fancy clothes—''

"Does that mean you're planning on arriving at

the chapel wearing nothing at all?" Evan was quick to ask, amusement lurking in his voice.

"Of course not," Jade shot back at him and felt her face grow hot. Why did she let him get to her so easily?

"I could lend you another one of my shirts," he teased, his blue eyes sparkling with humor.

Damn the man, Jade thought as she fought the impulse to return his smile. "Thank you, but that won't be necessary," she answered stiffly. "If there's nothing else, it's been a long day and I'm rather tired. I'll say good-night."

She turned to leave but his hand came up to stop her, accidentally brushing against her breast; a shiver of awareness spiraled through her. She jerked back as if she'd suddenly touched a live wire.

Evan's hand dropped to his side and a muscle jumped at his jaw. "I wanted to thank you for spending so much time with Matthew today. I don't think I've ever seen him this happy." The sincerity in Evan's voice only served to increase her confusion.

Her whole body was still humming from the brief but electrifying contact, and she couldn't quite bring herself to meet his gaze.

"Matthew's a great kid. He's easy to love," she said, sure Evan could hear the thunderous roar of her heartbeat.

"Then he's blessed indeed," Evan mumbled before tossing back the remainder of his brandy. "Good night, Jade." He crossed to the liquor cabinet and began to refill his glass.

Jade stood staring at Evan's back. What had he been thinking just then, she wondered. Was he already having second thoughts?

Chapter Seven

"How long will it take us to get there?" Matthew asked from the back seat of Evan's four by four.

"Once we're on Route 62, it will probably take a couple of hours to get to the Medford-Jackson County Airport," Evan replied.

Evan's truck, which had been safely housed in the garage throughout the worst of the storm, was equipped with snowtires and chains. Jade hadn't argued at Evan's choice of vehicle, knowing how ill equipped her own car had been in the snowy conditions.

Over a light breakfast, Evan had quickly gone over their itinerary and she'd been surprised to learn he'd already booked three seats on a flight back to Medford.

Their return flight was scheduled to leave San Francisco at seven in the evening, and while Jade was in some way relieved they wouldn't be staying overnight, she wasn't at all sure she shared his optimism at the outcome.

No new snow had fallen during the night and outside the sky was clear and the temperature a little above the freezing mark.

Evan turned on the radio and Jade was glad not to have to make conversation. She'd spent a sleepless night, her mind occupied with thoughts of Evan and what the future would bring.

After an early-morning shower, she'd decided to wear her old jeans and a warm sweater for the journey and hoped she'd have time to change into her black stretch pants and emerald green mohair sweater for the wedding ceremony.

Somehow it just didn't seem real that in a matter of a few hours she would become Evan's wife. Her heart skipped a beat at the thought and nervously she stole a glance at his handsome profile.

During the four months she and Evan had been engaged she'd often wiled away the lonely hours at the hotel dreaming about the day she'd walk down the aisle to be joined in holy wedlock to the man she'd loved with all her heart.

But that was then, and this was now. And the reason for this wedding had nothing whatsoever to do with the mutual love, respect and need two people had for each other, and everything to do with protecting a child from becoming a human pawn in a mercenary chess game.

Jade agreed with Evan. Matthew had suffered enough emotional upheaval, enough heartache in his young life when he'd lost his parents. And as Evan's wife, her purpose and presence at the hearing was simply to help undermine the Turners' case and hopefully sabotage their attempt to wrestle Matthew away from the one man he'd grown to love and trust.

Though there was no guarantee Evan's plan would work, Jade felt Evan's show of confidence was for Matthew's sake.

But what about after the hearing? The question had kept her awake for most of the long night.

When she'd agreed to become Evan's wife, she'd tossed in the condition that their marriage be a marriage in name only in a desperate attempt to erect some kind of barrier between them, knowing after the electrifying kiss they'd shared that the attraction she felt for Evan was as strong, if not stronger, than it had ever been.

Now she was slowly beginning to realize the price she would have to pay for her impulsiveness. But she'd painted herself into a corner. And much as she might want to retract the words and tell Evan she'd changed her mind, that she wasn't interested in a marriage without love, she couldn't bring herself to reject Matthew, not after the heartwarming and loving reception he'd afforded her.

A quick glance at Matthew buckled into the back seat confirmed he was busy with his crayons, coloring a picture.

Beside her, dressed somewhat formally in gray slacks, a blue shirt, silk patterned tie and navy sports jacket, Evan looked incredibly handsome and the picture of confidence.

A shiver ran through her as he leaned toward her to turn the heater on full blast. The warm air circulated through the cab and Jade soon began to feel drowsy.

"Jade, wake up." The velvetlike tones of Evan's voice drifted through to her, and Jade smiled as she nestled against something solid and warm.

She didn't want to wake up, didn't want to relinquish her dream, a dream where she and Evan had exchanged vows in front of the altar of a tiny chapel and Evan had just kissed her with a tenderness that had left her breathless and aching.

"Jade, wake up. We're here." Evan's voice was more urgent this time, effectively penetrating the foggy haze of her dream.

"What?" Jade sleepily opened her eyes. "Oh... I'm sorry." She bolted into a sitting position, realizing with a pang she'd been leaning against Evan's shoulder.

"No problem." Evan flashed her a brief smile, a smile that sent her pulse racing. "Matthew fell asleep, too," he told her. "Come on, sport, time to wake up." He tossed the words over his shoulder.

"How was the drive?" Jade asked. Glancing outside, she tried to get her bearings, but after a quick perusal of what appeared to be a large parking lot, nothing looked familiar.

"We made good time," Evan said as he turned off the engine. "The roads weren't as bad as I'd anticipated and there wasn't much traffic this morning."

"Where are we?" The question came from Matthew, who was unbuckling his seat belt.

"Medford Airport," Evan replied. "Matthew,

don't forget your backpack,'' he said as he opened the driver's side door.

Once inside the building, Evan checked in at the desk. A few minutes later he returned to say he'd managed to secure seats on an earlier flight, one that was already boarding. Hurrying to the departure gate, they quickly climbed the steps of the small plane that would fly them to Reno.

There was only two seats on either side of the narrow aisle. Matthew opted to sit with Jade, leaving Evan to occupy a seat several rows in front of them. The plane was soon airborne, and throughout the flight Jade was kept busy answering Matthew's questions and playing card games. She had little time to question the wisdom of what she was about to do.

It was a little before noon when the plane landed at Reno's busy airport, and as they followed their fellow passengers into the terminal, a sensation, like the brush of a hummingbird's wings, fluttered to life inside her.

With no luggage to collect from the carousel, Evan led them to the exit and once outside he strode toward the curb where a long black limousine was parked.

The sky above was cloudy but there was no snow on the ground, and in sharp contrast to the chilly weather they'd left behind, the temperature was a relatively mild fifty-eight degrees.

''Hop in,'' Evan said to Matthew when the limousine driver opened the passenger door.

''Wow…way cool!'' Matthew exclaimed as he scampered into the back of the large car.

Jade turned to Evan, but before she could comment or protest, he forestalled her.

"Taxi or limo, it makes no never mind," Evan said. "We're ahead of schedule and that means we can make a brief stop before we head to the chapel."

"A stop? Why? What for?" Jade asked.

"All in good time," came Evan's unhelpful reply. "Let's go, shall we?"

Jade joined Matthew in the back seat and Evan followed, opting for the seat facing her. As she sank back against the soft leather upholstery, their glances collided and Jade felt her heart begin to race.

Throughout the flight she'd wondered what thoughts were going through Evan's head with regard to their upcoming wedding, but if she'd expected to see a look of anxiety or apprehension in his eyes, she was doomed to disappointment.

Jade quickly turned her attention to Matthew, who was fiddling with the buttons on a panel in front of a small television screen on a table between the seats.

Glad of the distraction, Jade leaned over and quickly found the switch, but as the picture came into focus she felt the nervous quivering in her abdomen begin again.

Ten minutes later the limousine came to a halt at the curb and after instructing a contented Matthew to wait with the driver, Evan invited Jade to join him on the sidewalk.

Puzzled, Jade emerged from the vehicle and noticed they'd stopped in front of a row of shops, one of them a small boutique.

"I thought you might like something to wear

that's a little more in keeping with a wedding,'' he said as he ushered her into the store.

Jade wanted to protest, wanted to tell him it didn't matter what she wore, but the words wouldn't come, and in a small corner of her heart she was touched by his thoughtfulness.

Inside the store a smartly dressed woman came forward to greet them.

''Good morning. How may I help you?'' she asked.

''We're getting married in less than an hour,'' Evan said without preamble. ''Would you have something suitable for my fiancée...?''

''Hmm...well, let me see.'' The woman turned to study Jade for a moment. ''You have such lovely coloring,'' she commented. ''Yes, I believe I have just the outfit. Would you like to come this way?''

''But I—'' Jade began, stopping abruptly when Evan placed his hands on her shoulders and leaned toward her.

''Jade, we don't have time to argue. Please, just do it.'' He spoke the words softly into her ear and as his breath gently fanned her hair, Jade felt her body shiver in instant response.

''All right,'' she said, ducking away from him, hoping he hadn't noticed her quicksilver reaction to his nearness.

Ten minutes later Jade walked out of the dressing room wearing a stylishly cut dress and jacket in an exquisite shade of deep apricot that defined her slender figure and enhanced the orange and gold highlights in her hair.

''Here we are, sir. One blushing bride-to-be....''

said the cheerful saleslady. "I even found just the right shoes," she added, referring to the pair of shiny black pumps Jade now wore.

Jade held her breath as Evan turned to look at her. Her heart leapt into her throat as his gaze slowly traveled from her head to her toes and back up again.

For a fleeting moment a dark and dangerous expression flared to life in his eyes, sending a flurry of emotions rippling through her.

"And a beautiful bride-to-be at that," Evan said, a hint of huskiness in his voice.

For Jade, the hour that followed sped by in a blur. The limousine driver whisked them away, stopping only a scant five minutes later in front of a small chapel.

Once again Evan asked the driver to wait, but this time Matthew accompanied them inside. Jade remembered little of the ceremony, though she managed to give the correct response at the proper time and even summoned a smile as Evan slid a gold band onto the ring finger of her left hand.

The brush of Evan's lips on hers sent a tingling warmth through her, and the next thing she remembered was shaking hands with the man who'd performed the ceremony. Then Evan gently ushered her out to the limousine.

Half an hour later they boarded the flight to San Francisco and this time it was Matthew and Evan who sat together while Jade found herself in an aisle seat several rows behind them. She was married now, she mused. But everything still seemed quite unreal.

The plane was forced to stay in a holding pattern over San Francisco, and as a result their arrival was delayed. When they finally touched down on the tarmac Jade saw Evan continually check his watch, his impatience growing as he waited for the passengers ahead of him to disembark.

A line of taxis waited outside and before she'd even had time to notice that the sun was shining and the sky was a bright blue, they were heading downtown.

"Kelly, I'm sorry we're late," Evan said to the elegantly dressed young woman who came hurrying down the deserted hallway toward them.

After paying the taxi fare, Evan had herded Jade and Matthew through the large glass doors and into the building that housed Judge Andrew Mackenzie's office.

"I was beginning to think you'd missed the flight," she replied before turning to smile down at Matthew, who was holding on tight to Jade's left hand. "Hi, Matthew. How are you?" she asked, grinning at the boy, who smiled shyly back at her.

Evan moved closer to Jade and put his arm around her. "Kelly, I'd like you to meet…my wife, Jade. Jade, this is my lawyer, and friend, Kelly Nichols."

"It's nice to meet you." Jade managed to summon up a smile, more than a little surprised to discover Evan's lawyer was a very attractive young woman.

"The pleasure is all mine," Kelly said, extending her hand. "Oh, and by the way, congratulations!"

she added. "Well, if you're ready, we'd better go right in. They're waiting for us."

At Kelly's words Jade's heart skipped a beat. She threw a quick nervous glance at Evan, who smiled reassuringly at her, sending her pulse tripping over itself in confusion.

Evan's hand on the middle of her back gently urged her forward, and fighting down the panic suddenly assailing her, she walked toward the door of the office.

In the waiting room the receptionist smiled a greeting before rising to knock on the oak door behind her. Moments later she disappeared inside.

Jade's nervous gaze flew to the three people seated on the moss green leather sofa nearby.

"Matthew, you poor sweet darling boy. Come over here and let me look at you," said the dark-haired woman sitting at one end of the sofa. "Surely you haven't forgotten your Aunt Baba?" she added, throwing a hostile and accusing glance in Evan's direction.

Matthew immediately buried his face against Jade's dress, clinging to her as if he might never let go. At the child's reaction, Jade saw Barbara Turner's mouth tighten into a thin line. She glared at Evan, anger and resentment in her eyes.

Jade put her free hand on Matthew's shoulder. "Don't be shy, Matthew," she coaxed, though she felt sure Matthew's reaction had been generated by fear rather than shyness. "Say hello to your aunt and uncle," she said.

"Hello." Matthew tossed the word over his

shoulder, but before Barbara Turner could respond, the receptionist reappeared.

"Judge Mackenzie will see you all now," she announced from the open doorway.

For a tense moment no one moved. It was Evan who broke the silence. "Well, darling. Let's get this farce over with, shall we?" With that, he captured Jade's hand in his and, giving Matthew a gentle nudge, he and Jade made their way across the carpeted room.

As they swept past the threesome seated on the leather sofa, Jade glimpsed a look of shock on Barbara Turner's face.

Judge Mackenzie, a robust man in his sixties with graying hair and a matching full beard, sat behind a large oak desk strewn with papers. The sweet scent of pipe tobacco permeated the room.

"Please sit down," said the judge.

Jade nodded and chose the chair next to the wall, making room for Matthew beside her. Evan moved to stand behind her while Kelly occupied a chair next to Jade.

The Turners and their lawyer opted for the chairs on the other side of the room.

"Now, then. Who would like to begin the discussion?" the judge asked once everyone was settled.

"With due respect, Judge Mackenzie," Kelly Nichols was quick to jump in, "my client wishes me to state he resents very much the fact he had to come here today to defend his guardianship of Matthew. For the past year he has provided a loving and stable environment for the boy and can see no reason for his guardianship to be challenged.''

"Thank you, Miss Nichols. Your protest is duly noted," said the judge before turning to the man standing behind the Turners. ''Mr. Barnard?''

"Your Honor, my clients feel Matthew does not receive the kind of care a boy of his age needs, especially when Mr. Mathieson's career takes him away on assignment for days and sometimes weeks at a time."

The judge turned to Evan. ''Mr. Mathieson?''

"Your Honor, I took a two-month leave of absence from my job when Matthew first came to live with me. We both had adjustments to make and I feel we bonded well during that time. After I returned to work I hired a live-in housekeeper for those times when I was away. But I've been cutting back substantially on assignments that take me out of town and away from Matthew," Evan explained.

"Your Honor—" Barbara Turner joined the discussion "—leaving that poor sweet young boy in the care of a housekeeper for days at a time is, to my mind, simply a crime. He needs the kind of stable and loving home environment my husband and I can provide—"

"Your Honor," Evan cut in. ''Matthew already has a stable and loving environment with my wife and me.''

"Wife? This…is your wife?" Barbara Turner said with a scathing look at Jade. ''How convenient!'' she added, her face growing red.

"Mrs. Turner, please," Judge Mackenzie cautioned.

"But Your Honor, this is outrageous." Barbara Turner continued, ignoring the judge's warning. "Why don't you ask him how long he's been married, because he certainly didn't have a wife a month ago or a week ago, for that matter," she spat out. "Can't you see he's desperate? So desperate, he'll do anything, even try to pass this...this floozy off as his wife, just to keep Matthew."

"Barbara..." Alex Turner put his hand on his wife's arm, only to have it flung off.

"I bet they're not even married," she blundered on. "I bet he paid her to play the part of his wife. But he doesn't fool me, not for one moment."

Stunned by the woman's arrogance and bitterness, Jade could no longer endure the insults being tossed at her and Evan.

"May I respond to that, Judge Mackenzie?" Jade kept her tone even while her heart was pounding away.

"By all means," the judge replied as he leaned back in his chair.

"Evan and I are married. I have the papers right here to prove it." She patted her purse. "I grant you we've only been married a very short time, but we've known each other a lot longer and I deeply resent Mrs. Turner's accusations.

"Evan and I love Matthew as if he were our own son," she continued with sincerity. "We are a family, a real family, and we came here today to ask that you allow us to remain a family."

"How touching," Barbara Turner said softly, her voice heavy with sarcasm.

"Thank you, Mrs. Mathieson," Judge Mackenzie

said, ignoring Barbara Turner's comment. "Well, Matthew?" he added, turning his attention to the boy. "What about you? Are you happy living with—" he paused to glance down at the file on his desk "—Evan and Jade?" he finished, giving the boy an encouraging smile.

"They've probably coached him and told him what to say," Barbara Turner muttered scornfully before Matthew could even respond.

Judge Mackenzie pulled off his glasses and leaned forward to rest his elbows on his desk. "Mrs. Turner, unless I address you directly, please refrain from making any more comments. Thank you."

Matthew turned to glance up at Evan, then at Jade. "I like it a lot," he said. "I miss my mom and dad…but Evan says he misses them, too, and we talk about them sometimes." Matthew stopped and Jade put her arm around his shoulder and gave him a squeeze, fighting back tears.

"Evan's teaching me to play chess," Matthew hurried on, changing the subject. "And we're a real family now, like it was with my mom and dad." He stopped and the silence that ensued was electric.

"Thank you, Matthew," Judge Mackenzie said after a lengthy pause.

"Judge Mackenzie, surely you aren't—" Barbara Turner began.

"Mrs. Turner," the judge cut in, his tone icy, "I don't know what strings you pulled to orchestrate this meeting and I don't want to know," he quickly asserted. "But in any event it is my recommendation Matthew remain in the care and custody of Evan

Mathieson and his wife, Jade, who appear to be doing a very good job of raising this young boy.''

''But you can't—'' Barbara Turner began.

''I assure you, Mrs. Turner, I can,'' Judge Mackenzie responded in a decisive tone that left no room for further argument.

''Does that mean I get to stay with Evan and Jade?'' Matthew asked, obviously confused by the judge's comments.

''Yes, Matthew, it does,'' the judge replied with a warm smile.

Matthew emitted a triumphant yell and, jumping down from the chair, threw himself at Evan.

Feelings of relief and joy sprinted through Jade and she turned to smile at Evan, who had lifted the boy into his arms. Jade felt her heart skip a beat when she saw the glint of moisture in Evan's blue eyes.

His smiling gaze collided with hers, and in that fleeting second Jade was struck with the stunning realization she still loved Evan…had never stopped loving him.

Chapter Eight

Barbara and Alex Turner, followed by their lawyer, stormed out of the judge's office without as much as a backward glance or a goodbye to Matthew.

Evan lowered Matthew to the floor and, after shaking hands with Judge Mackenzie, exited the office. Wanting to avoid the possibility of running into the Turners, they slowly made their way from the building.

"Thanks for everything, Kelly," Evan said as they spilled out into the street. Outside, the sky was steadily growing dark and some streetlights had already come on.

"You deserve the credit, Evan—you and Jade," Kelly responded. "But you'll still be getting a bill from me," she added with a cheeky grin. "I've got to run. Can I drop you folks off anywhere?"

"Thanks, but we're going to find a restaurant and have a bite to eat," Evan replied.

"Then I'll say goodbye." Kelly stretched up to give Evan a kiss, then turned to smile at Jade and Matthew who were standing nearby. "It was great to see you again, Matthew, and a pleasure to meet you, too, Jade. Evan's a lucky man. Ciao!" With a wave she hurried off down the street.

"I think we should celebrate. Where would you like to eat, Matthew?" Evan asked.

"Can I have a hamburger and fries?"

"That sounds like a great idea!" Evan said. "What do you say, Jade?"

"Fine, but shouldn't we be heading back to the airport?" Jade responded, recalling Evan had made arrangements to catch a flight back to Medford.

"We have plenty of time," Evan calmly assured her. "If my memory serves me well there's a great little hamburger place not far from here," he went on. "What do you say we give it a try?"

"Yeah!" Matthew eagerly agreed.

"Let's walk, shall we," Evan suggested. "It's a nice evening and we don't have to plow our way through snow," he added with a grin.

The restaurant was only a few blocks away. As they approached the building Jade saw what looked like the front end of a pink Cadillac protruding from the rooftop.

"Wow! Look! There's a car on the roof," Matthew said, pointing excitedly.

Evan grinned and nodded. "Cool, huh?"

The parking lot was busy and from inside came the sounds of sixties rock music. Once through the glass doors the noise level rose considerably, but the atmosphere was cheery and the clientele appeared to be made up of families with young children, and small groups of teenagers.

A waitress led them to a table in the corner near an old jukebox. Matthew couldn't take his eyes off the jukebox and watched in fascination as another young patron dropped in a coin and punched the buttons.

"Hey, Matthew. Want to put some quarters in the jukebox and pick out a few tunes?" Evan asked a few minutes later once the waitress had taken their order.

"Okay," Matthew replied, hopping eagerly off his chair. "Which tunes will I pick?" he asked as Evan dug in his pants pocket.

"It doesn't matter." Evan gave Matthew a small handful of quarters, smiling after the boy as he scampered to the jukebox nearby.

"You're quiet, Jade. Is anything wrong?" Evan's softly spoken question startled her.

She forced herself to smile but deliberately avoided making eye contact with Evan, fearful he would see the turmoil raging inside her. Since leaving the judge's office, she was still trying to come to terms with the knowledge that her feelings for Evan were as strong and as real as ever.

"I'm fine," she lied. "Relieved it's all over, I guess," she added as she fiddled with her napkin and rearranged the cutlery on the table.

When Evan's hand reached over to cover hers, a jolt of awareness sprinted up her arm to spread quickly through her, intensifying the tangle her emotions were already in.

She jerked free of his touch and tried to ignore

the way her pulse was racing. It took every ounce of control to meet his eyes. Concern and something more shone in their depths and she noticed his handsome features were marred by a puzzled frown.

"There's something troubling you, Jade," he insisted. "If I can, I'd like to help," he added as he withdrew his hand.

"I'm not altogether sure you needed me there today," Jade said, voicing the doubt that had been nagging at her since leaving the judge's office.

Evan silently wove his fingers together in front of him. "The threat of losing Matthew was very real, and not something I was prepared to take lightly," he countered in a steely voice.

"As a married couple we presented a united front," Evan went on. "Your impassioned speech, together with Matthew's own endorsement of being part of a real family again, all contributed to convincing the judge to rule in our favor. Believe me, if you hadn't been there today the outcome could have been quite different."

There was more than a hint of exasperation in his voice and, glancing across the table at him, Jade caught the glimmer of another emotion in the depths of his eyes.

His tone was sincere, his argument persuasive, and in a corner of her heart she knew he was right, but it did little to alleviate the pain vibrating through her, a pain brought on by the knowledge that while he'd married her as a safeguard against losing Matthew, she'd married Evan because she still loved him with all her heart.

"There's something else. What is it?" Evan asked gently. "Can't you tell me?"

Jade met his gaze once more and for a heart-stopping second the temptation to blurt out the truth, to say the three words that were playing like a broken record inside her head, was almost more than she could resist.

Suddenly Matthew's excited voice cut through the silence.

"The hamburgers are coming! The hamburgers are coming!"

Jade drew a startled breath and darted a glance to the source of the voice in time to see Matthew dodge in front of the waitress, who was bearing down on them with three large platters.

As Matthew clambered onto his chair, the raucous tones of Mick Jagger shouting that he couldn't get any satisfaction boomed out over the restaurant.

After the waitress withdrew, Jade deliberately kept her attention on the food on her plate. The appetizing scent of freshly cooked hamburgers had her mouth watering, and she was surprised to discover she was hungry.

As she bit down on a piping hot French fry, she sent up a silent prayer of thanks that she hadn't succumbed to the temptation to declare her true feelings and make a complete and utter fool of herself.

Throughout their engagement, whenever she'd voiced her feelings or expressed her love, Evan had rarely reciprocated with those three magical words, *I love you.* Instead, he'd murmured, "Me, too," or "Likewise."

At first Jade hadn't minded, and on occasion had

teased him, but as time went on she'd been hard-pressed to ignore the empty feeling inside.

Reflecting back over their four months together, she suddenly wondered if the reason he hadn't told her he loved her was because he *hadn't* loved her, or at least hadn't been capable of loving her as totally and completely as she'd loved him. If that had indeed been the case, breaking their engagement had been the kindest thing to do.

And it only seemed logical to conclude that if he hadn't loved her then it was unlikely his feelings for her had changed. Telling Evan she still loved him would serve no real purpose and simply create more tension between them.

Matthew's happiness and emotional well-being were Evan's top priority, and not for the first time, Jade found herself wondering if he would still have broken their engagement had he known she was carrying his child.

But it was much too late to play the what-if game and she was wise enough to know there was no going back; the past couldn't be changed. She would just have to learn to keep her emotions under wraps and pour all her love on Matthew.

The hamburgers proved to be as delicious as Evan had predicted and to her relief Matthew's random choice of music from the jukebox made it impossible to carry on a conversation.

''That was great,'' Evan said as he used his napkin to wipe his hands. ''While you two finish up, I'll confirm our flight.'' Pushing his chair back he rose from the table.

''This sure is a neat place,'' Matthew said, his

face all smiles as he dipped the last of his fries into the blob of ketchup on his plate.

"Mmm...you're right about that," Jade commented.

"More coffee, ma'am?" asked the waitress as she approached the table carrying a glass carafe.

"Yes, thank you," Jade responded.

"Would your husband like a refill, too?" the waitress asked.

"Ah...yes...I think so, please." Jade stumbled over the words and felt her face grow warm, caught off guard by the waitress's reference to her husband. Somehow it didn't seem real.

"Would anyone like dessert?" the waitress added once she'd refilled Evan's coffee cup.

Jade saw Matthew's eyes widen with obvious interest as he turned to give her a pleading look.

"Our ice cream is homemade and we have every flavor imaginable," the waitress continued.

"May I have some chocolate ice cream, please," Matthew asked politely.

Jade didn't have the heart to refuse. Evan had said they were celebrating. "I don't see why not," she said, and was rewarded with a winning smile.

The waitress glanced at Jade.

"Nothing for me, thank you," she said, noticing Evan winding his way toward them, a thoughtful expression on his face.

"Want some ice cream?" Matthew asked as Evan slid into the chair opposite. "I'm having chocolate."

"Chocolate for me, too," Evan said, and the waitress nodded and withdrew.

"Something wrong?" Jade asked.

"The flight to Medford has been canceled," Evan said.

"Canceled?" Jade repeated. "But—"

"Medford Airport has been closed due to high winds and blowing snow," he explained.

"Does that mean we have to stay here all night?" Matthew was quick to ask.

"That's right," Evan replied.

"But I didn't bring my pajamas," Matthew said, his tone serious.

Evan's low chuckle sent Jade's pulse racing and her eyes flicked to meet his in time to see the twinkle of humor in their depths. "Me, either," he said, holding her gaze for several long seconds.

"Where are we going to sleep?" Matthew wanted to know. The question effectively distracted Jade and helped defuse the tension arcing between them.

"In a hotel, of course," Evan told him. "I've just reserved a suite at the Hyatt in the Embarcadero Center, not far from here," he added, undoubtedly for her benefit.

"A suite? What's that?" Matthew asked with a puzzled frown.

"A suite is like a small apartment. It has a couple of bedrooms, a living room and several bathrooms," Evan patiently explained.

"I stayed in a hotel once with my mom and dad," Matthew informed them. "We had one room with two big beds in it. They slept in one bed and I slept in the other bed," he explained. "Is that what we're going to do?" he asked innocently.

To Jade's relief the waitress chose that moment to reappear. After serving the ice cream, she produced the check from the pocket of her apron and dropped it on the table.

"There's no hurry, sir," she said with a smile. "Just whenever you're ready."

Fifteen minutes later they left, and under the dazzling lights of the restaurant's neon sign, Evan hailed a cruising taxi. Throughout the drive to the hotel, Jade willed herself not to think about the night's sleeping arrangements.

Evan unlocked the door to the suite located on the eighteenth floor and Matthew rushed inside, eager to explore their new and temporary surroundings.

He scooted in and out of the bathroom, the first room on the right, before running across the hall and into one of the bedrooms.

Jade came to a halt in the doorway and, reaching in, switched on the light.

"Can I sleep in here?" Matthew asked from atop the queen-size bed.

"Sure," Evan said as he came up behind Jade.

"Wait! You said there were two bedrooms. I want to see the other one first." Matthew jumped off the bed and ran toward them at breakneck speed.

Jade took a quick step back to avoid a collision, an action that brought her up against Evan's solid frame. She gasped softly at the contact, and all at once her legs felt like two strands of wool as a familiar weakness assailed her.

"Sorry," she managed to murmur, trying to ignore the frisson of heat streaking through her as Evan's hands came up to steady her.

"Any time," Evan said, his breath fanning the hair at the nape of her neck. "Oh…and just to put you at ease, I'll be sleeping on the pullout bed in the living room."

"Thank you," Jade said huskily. Breaking free of his hold she followed Matthew into the second bedroom.

"This room's bigger and it has a bathroom," Matthew announced as he came running into the hall. "But I like the other room best. It has a bigger TV," he went on.

"Then it's yours, sport," Evan declared before moving past the door and into the spacious living room decorated in vivid blues and greens.

"Wow! Look at all the twinkling lights," Matthew said as he joined Evan and ran to the large window that afforded a view of the San Francisco skyline.

"Ah…I'm going to take a long leisurely bath," Jade said.

Evan turned to look at her.

"By all means," he said.

"Can I watch TV?" Matthew asked, already moving to the coffee table where he picked up the remote control.

"Okay, but only for half an hour," Evan told him in a voice that brooked no argument.

Matthew scrunched up his face in obvious disapproval, but he made no comment as he hopped onto the couch.

Jade made her way to the master bedroom, retrieving the boutique shopping bag that contained her slacks and sweater.

Closing the bedroom door behind her, she leaned against it for a moment and let out a tired sigh. It had been a long day, an unusual day, an unforgettable day. Her wedding day.

As she dropped the bag on the bed, the gold band on the fourth finger of her left hand winked at her and she froze. Her dream had come true. She was Mrs. Evan Mathieson, Evan's wife, but the joy and happiness she should have been feeling was sadly lacking.

She'd been surprised when Evan had produced the ring from his jacket pocket at the chapel, but she'd been too dazed to give it much more than a passing thought. On reflection it seemed unusual for him to be carrying around a ring.

Jade twisted the gold band and noticed, with a start, that it appeared to be engraved. With a trembling hand she slid the ring from her finger, for closer inspection. Her heart shuddered to a standstill and a pain sliced through her when she read the inscription. Forever Yours.

Had the ring been meant for someone else? The thought filled her with quiet despair, and for a moment she couldn't move or breathe. The question continued to spin inside her head but she had no way of finding out the answer, not unless she asked Evan himself.

With a heavy heart Jade returned the gold band to her finger and slowly begun to undress. After rinsing her underclothes and hanging them to dry, she climbed into the bathtub, hoping the hot water would soothe her battered emotions.

Twenty minutes later Jade decided she'd been

moping in the tub long enough. The bath had done little to ease the tension throbbing inside her.

She dried herself with a big bath towel, and after carefully brushing out her hair, she put on the cream colored terry-cloth bathrobe hanging up in the bathroom and returned to the bedroom.

"Jade!"

Evan's urgent call accompanied by a sharp knock on the bedroom door startled her. Tightening the belt on her robe, she quickly crossed to the door.

"Sorry to bother you," Evan said. "Matthew's been throwing up again," he announced, concern etched on his face. "He's been asking for you. Would you mind sitting with him while I call downstairs and see if I can get a doctor to come and take a look at him?"

"Of course," Jade replied and followed Evan to the second bedroom.

Matthew lay under the bedcovers, his face flushed, his eyes tearful. As Jade crossed to the bed Matthew burst into tears and she immediately gathered him into her arms.

"Aw…sweetheart. It's all right. Don't cry," Jade soothed as she gently rocked him.

"I—I—I—was si-sick—again…" Matthew stammered as he pulled away to sniff noisily.

Jade reached for the box of tissues on the bedside table, noticing that Evan had already withdrawn.

"Blow," Jade said, handing him several tissues. Matthew did as she instructed, then snuggled against her once again.

"Where's Evan?" Matthew asked. "What's he doing?"

"He's calling the front desk to ask if there's a doctor in the hotel who can come and take a look at you," Jade answered. "Here he is," she added as Evan, his face a tight mask of control, reentered the bedroom.

"Hey, sport. How are you feeling?" Evan moved to sit on the opposite side of the bed from Jade.

"Okay," Matthew replied in a small voice.

"There's a doctor on his way up to take a look at you," Evan told him.

"I won't have to go to the hospital, will I?" Matthew asked a little fearfully. "My friend Adam had to go to hospital when he got sick."

"I don't think so," Evan replied in a reassuring voice. "But we'll wait and see what the doctor has to say."

"It's probably all the excitement you've had today," Jade suggested. "I bet you'll feel better in the morning."

A few minutes later they heard a knock on the outer door and Evan went to answer it. He returned, accompanied by a young man of about thirty-five dressed in casual attire and carrying a small black briefcase.

"Dr. Kent, I'd like you to meet my wife, Jade," Evan said. "And your patient's name is Matthew."

Dr. Kent nodded to Jade before turning his attention to Matthew.

"Well, Matthew. What seems to be the problem?" Dr. Kent asked as he set his briefcase on the bed.

"I had a sore tummy and I threw up," Matthew told him as he pushed himself into a sitting position in order to get a closer look inside the doctor's open briefcase. "What's that?" Matthew asked with more curiosity than fear when he saw the instrument in Dr. Kent's hand.

"It's a thermometer," the doctor replied. "I'm going to put this in your ear and take your temperature. All right?"

"Okay," Matthew said.

Dr. Kent proceeded to give Matthew an examination, and when he was finished he smiled reassuringly at the boy.

"Well, Matthew, you do have a slight temperature," said Dr. Kent, "but I don't think there's any need for concern." He turned to address Evan and Jade. "I would suggest however, that you take your son to see your family doctor when you get home." He smiled once more at Matthew. "In the meantime, Matthew, I think you should get some sleep, and take it easy on your tummy tomorrow. Okay?"

"Okay," Matthew responded.

"Thank you, Dr. Kent," Evan responded. "We appreciate you coming to take a look."

"No problem," said the doctor as he snapped his briefcase closed. "Good evening," he added, and followed Evan from the bedroom.

"Jade, can you stay with me for a while?" Matthew asked in a small voice.

"Sure," she replied with a smile.

"I don't like being sick," Matthew said as he slid down beneath the bedcovers once more.

Jade smiled. "I don't think anyone likes being sick," she replied as she tucked the covers around him.

"It's been quite a day," Evan said as he rejoined them. "Flying here and there and going to see the judge," he commented, obviously feeling Matthew's tummy upset might have been the result of feelings of anxiety.

"I've never been to a wedding before or seen a judge," Matthew replied. "I liked the wedding part best," he added with a smile. "Jade looked pretty, didn't she, Evan?"

"She did indeed," came the instant response, the low timbre of his voice as potent as any caress.

"Did you like the wedding part, Jade?" Matthew asked.

Jade's mouth suddenly went dry. "Yes…the wedding was very nice," she managed to respond.

"Dr. Kent thought you guys were my mom and dad, didn't he?" Matthew said with a grin.

Jade threw a fleeting glance at Evan and saw an emotion flicker in his eyes before he quickly controlled it.

"Yes, he did," Evan answered evenly. "But that's an easy mistake for people to make," he continued. "Does it bother you?"

"No…" Matthew replied after a brief hesitation. "I mean, a bit, I guess, but I don't mind, 'cause we are a family now, right?"

Evan smiled and leaned over to drop a kiss on Matthew's head. "Right," he confirmed and playfully ruffled Matthew's hair. "I think we've all had enough excitement for one day. It's time for you to get some sleep. Good night, Matthew," Evan said. "We'll leave the door open and if you need us, just yell! Okay?"

"Okay," Matthew said. "Night, Evan. Night, Jade."

The lump of emotion clogging Jade's throat made it almost impossible for her to reply. "Night, Matthew," she whispered huskily as she bent to kiss his cheek.

Moments later Jade and Evan were standing in the hallway but as Jade made to return to the master bedroom, Evan stopped her.

"There are a couple of things we need to discuss," Evan said. "I was wondering if you'd like to join me for a nightcap?"

Jade's first instinct was to refuse, but there was something, a hint of a plea perhaps in his voice that tugged strangely at her heart.

"All right," she heard herself say, instantly regretting her decision when she remembered she was naked beneath the bathrobe.

Chapter Nine

"Would you like a glass of wine?" Evan asked as he crossed to the bar.

"I'd prefer water, please," Jade responded, thinking she needed to keep her wits about her.

"There's mineral water," Evan suggested over his shoulder.

"Fine," Jade said, moving to the easy chair, deliberately choosing it instead of the couch, for the simple reason she wanted to avoid having Evan sit next to her.

"One mineral water," Evan said a few moments later as he handed her a glass.

"Thank you," Jade said, and felt her body tense as his fingers made fleeting contact with hers. "What is it you wanted to talk to me about?" she asked before taking a sip.

"What was your impression of Barbara and Alex

Turner?'' he countered, evading her question by asking one of his own.

Jade was silent for a long moment. ''They certainly didn't seem the least bit interested in Matthew,'' she said at last.

''They didn't even bother to say goodbye to him,'' Evan said scornfully.

''I can't help feeling sorry for them,'' Jade added, staring at him thoughtfully over the rim of her glass.

''Then you have a generous heart,'' Evan commented as he perched on the arm of the couch nearest to her chair.

At his compliment Jade felt her face grow warm and she quickly took a sip of water, hoping Evan wouldn't notice the color rising in her cheeks. But he was watching her, those blue eyes of his missing nothing.

''They are his aunt and uncle, and there are really no winners in these kinds of situations. Everyone loses, even Matthew,'' Jade said. ''He's lucky he has you on his side.''

''Now he has both of us,'' Evan amended.

Jade shifted uncomfortably in the chair and crossed one leg over the other. ''You wanted to talk to me?'' she repeated, hoping to redirect the conversation.

Evan's gaze drifted to the spot where Jade's robe had slid off her knee to reveal the milky white smoothness of her thighs.

Desire curled its hot fist inside him, catching him momentarily off guard, and in an attempt to combat the need suddenly stampeding through him, he brought the wineglass to his mouth, giving all his concentration to its crisp bouquet.

He sipped the scented Chardonnay but it did little to alleviate the tension tightening his body.

"How flexible do you think Veronica will be about your job once she knows we're married?" Evan asked.

Jade was silent. Everything had happened so fast, she hadn't given much thought to how her marriage to Evan would affect her job.

"I don't think there'll be a problem," Jade replied. "Apart from paying a visit to the office now and then, I work out of my apartment most of the time, unless I'm researching or doing interviews. All I need is my laptop, a phone and a fax-modem and I can access the magazine whenever I need to."

"So moving to Boston won't create too much upheaval," Evan went on.

"I shouldn't think so," Jade replied, ignoring the shiver of apprehension that danced down her spine at the thought of living anywhere with Evan. "But I do plan to continue working," she told him, wanting to state her position from the outset.

"I don't recall asking you to quit," Evan said, an edge to his voice. "Matthew is in school, and arranging a schedule around that shouldn't be a problem."

"How's he doing in school?" Jade asked.

"He loves it," Evan replied. "He wasn't too happy about being pulled out of class to come on this trip."

"Did you tell him what the Turners were trying to do?" she asked, curiosity getting the better of her.

"Yes," Evan answered. "I felt it was his right to know the truth…just in case…" His voice trailed off.

"So Matthew knew the Turners were trying to take him away from you," Jade said.

"Yes, he knew," Evan replied. "And he trusted me not to let it happen," he added with a sigh. "I couldn't let him down."

"You didn't," Jade said, all the while thinking Matthew's faith in Evan had undoubtedly intensified the pressure he'd been under, forcing him to take drastic measures—such as marrying a woman he didn't love in order to ensure Matthew's emotional security.

"When do you have to be back in Boston?" Jade asked.

Evan took another sip of his wine before answering. "Not till next week," he replied, refraining from adding that his contract with the television station was up for renewal, and for the past month he'd been seriously looking into other options, including relocation to the West Coast.

His father wasn't getting any younger, and ever since Matthew had entered the picture, Hank had been pestering Evan to move back to Oregon so that Hank could be a grandfather to the boy.

His father had also mentioned he was thinking of retiring, a subject his father liked to talk about often and at great length. But when Hank asked if Evan knew of anyone who might be interested in managing the two newspapers he owned, he'd succeeded in planting an idea in Evan's head, the idea that he might like to take on the challenge himself.

Now that the hearing was behind him, Evan resolved to have a long talk with his father on the
subject.

"Evan?" Jade's soft voice cut through his musings.

"Sorry…" Evan flashed an apologetic smile.
"I've got rather a lot on my mind." He leaned forward to rest his forearms on his thighs, cupping his
wineglass in both hands.

"Matthew will be fine," Jade said, obviously believing he'd been thinking about the boy. "He's
probably still a little stressed by all that happened
today."

Evan met her gaze. "I hope you're right," he
answered, touched by her concern. "It amazes me
how quickly one small child can climb inside your
heart and take up residence."

Pain tore through Jade at the depth of emotion
she could hear in his voice, and she quickly looked
away. She'd often wondered how Evan would have
felt about their child had the baby survived. Now
she knew.

"Being a parent is one of the hardest jobs I've
ever had to do," Evan continued, his tone sincere.

"I'd say you're doing a great job," Jade said,
praying Evan wouldn't notice the huskiness in her
voice.

"I just wish it hadn't been necessary…that Nina
and Philip were still here." With a ragged sigh Evan
lowered his head to stare silently into his wineglass.

Jade felt her eyes sting with tears and resolutely
she blinked them away. Slumped over, Evan looked
the picture of desolation, as if the whole world were

somehow resting on his shoulders, and she had to fight the longing to reach out and touch him.

"I suppose you know your father's talking about retiring again," Jade commented in an attempt to distract him.

"What…? Oh…yes, he did mention it," Evan said as he pulled himself erect. "I think he might even be serious this time," he added, rising to his feet.

"He always sounds serious," Jade said lightly, drawing a smile from Evan.

"One of these days he just might surprise us," Evan remarked before moving to the bar to refill his glass. "I appreciate the fact that you've been keeping an eye on him," he said turning to face her once more. "So, tell me, where *did* you run off to when you left New Orleans?"

Jade's heartbeat raced at the question and she quickly looked down at the empty glass in her hands. "I…" She swallowed the emotion clogging her throat. "I flew to L.A. and stayed there for a few weeks," she told him truthfully.

"Is that where you met Veronica?" he asked, his tone casual.

"Yes," Jade responded before going on to elaborate on that first meeting with her boss, who'd happened to be staying at the same hotel in L.A.

Jade told Evan how Veronica had advised her to take the courses she needed to complete her degree, then come see her about a job. After returning to Portland, Jade had taken Veronica's advice. She'd felt a deep sense of accomplishment and pride when she'd landed a job with the magazine.

For the next hour, conversation between them flowed from one subject to another and Jade found it both invigorating and challenging keeping mentally abreast of a man of Evan's intelligence.

During their four months together Evan had enjoyed teasing her, drawing her into arguments that were for the most part light and trivial. While their verbal jousting had been fun, more often than not it had merely been a prelude to lovemaking.

Jade suddenly realized that they'd rarely spent an evening like this, exchanging ideas and opinions, exploring each other's minds, discussing topics of mutual interest, getting to know each other better.

"Look at the time," Evan said, rising from the depths of the couch where he'd been lounging for the past hour. "It's been a long day. You must be tired. I know I am," he added.

Jade glanced at the digital clock on the bar, surprised to discover it was well past ten. Rising from the chair, she tightened the sash on her robe.

"I'll check on Matthew," she said.

"I was about to do the same," Evan responded and, setting his empty wineglass on the nearest table, he caught up with her.

Evan eased open the door to Matthew's bedroom, and like two doting parents they tiptoed across the carpeted floor to stand on either side of the bed.

In the shadowed darkness of the room Jade could see Matthew had thrown off the bedcovers and lay sprawled across the queen-size bed looking small and very vulnerable.

With gentle fingers she brushed a stray lock of

dark hair from Matthew's forehead, and though his skin felt warm to the touch, he wasn't unduly hot.

Jade pulled the covers over Matthew before retracing her steps. On reaching the doorway she turned to wish Evan good-night, only to find him directly behind her.

Their bodies collided and Jade's heart leapt into her throat when his blue eyes locked on hers. The air between them crackled with tension, and before she even had a chance to draw breath his mouth swooped down to claim hers in a kiss that catapulted her, in one swift soundless second, to the edge of reason.

A need she'd long denied herself exploded like a firecracker inside her, setting off a chain reaction throughout her body that left her burning with desire, a desire only this man could satisfy.

She'd almost forgotten the hot and heady taste of him and the havoc his mouth could so easily arouse. Her heart was thumping like a bass drum against her breast and her head was reeling from the shock of a thousand tiny explosions.

When she felt his hand slip beneath the folds of her robe to gently cup her breast, a white-hot heat spiraled through her, sweeping even the thought of resistance aside.

Evan's mind blurred as his senses overdosed on the woman in his arms. He hadn't meant to start this, but the scent of lilacs swirling around him was making him dizzy with need. The seductive taste of desire on her lips was itself a powerful aphrodisiac. The silky smoothness of her breast as it lay in the palm of his hand fired up his blood, arousing him unbearably, and her soft sigh of surrender was sweet music to his ears.

Jade's hands found their way around Evan's neck to urge him closer, and when she felt his fingers feather across her shoulder to push aside her robe, she moaned softly into his mouth arching against him as a passion she'd all but forgotten threatened to overwhelm her.

He couldn't seem to get enough of her, and as he explored the smooth planes of her back and slid his hands over her firm rounded bottom, he almost lost it.

Raising his mouth from Jade's, Evan drew a steadying breath, grimly holding on as he fought for control. He could hear the thunderous roar of his pulse, feel his heart pounding like a jackhammer as he struggled to rein in the passion tearing through him.

Slowly he released the breath he was holding, but when he opened his eyes and saw the reflection of his own desire burning in Jade's eyes it was all he could do not to lift her into his arms and carry her into the bedroom.

"Jade?" His voice was a hoarse whisper of need. "You know I want you—" He broke off, his breathing ragged. "But before this gets totally out of hand, I want to be sure it's what you want, too."

Evan's comment acted like a splash of cold water on Jade. She gasped and pulled away, horrified at her wanton reaction to his kiss and angry with herself for not putting up even a token resistance.

Twisting away, she wrapped the folds of her robe around her, tying the belt with trembling fingers.

"No...it's not what I want," she said, her voice wavering as she fought to suppress the need vibrating through her. Her body, however, continued to cry out for the fulfillment only he could give, a mocking testimony to the lie she'd just spoken.

Resolutely she reminded herself she'd been down this road before. And she'd learned the hard way that desire alone just wasn't enough; it would never be enough.

She wanted it all.

"Then I'd advise you to escape now," Evan said in a voice devoid of emotion.

With as much dignity as she could muster, Jade made her way down the dimly lit hallway, fighting back tears, telling herself she'd been a fool to agree to marry Evan in the first place and a bigger fool to think she would ever be content in a marriage of convenience, a marriage without love.

Evan watched Jade disappear into the master bedroom. Muttering a few well-chosen curses, he returned to the living room and, raking a hand through his hair, strode to the window.

Fool! He silently berated himself as he gazed unseeing at the twinkling lights spread out below. Why had he stopped? Why hadn't he just carried her into the bedroom and taken what she'd been eager and willing to give?

Because she would have hated him in the morning, that's why, a small voice inside his head responded. And because he would have hated himself more.

To wake up and have Jade staring at him, her eyes

silently accusing, blaming him for taking advantage of her in a moment of weakness, would have been too much to bear.

But he had only himself to blame. He should never have let her go, never have broken their engagement. He'd been an arrogant fool to think he'd had the right to decide what was best for Jade without even bothering to consult her.

All he'd seen was her unhappiness, an unhappiness that seemed to deepen with each passing day. Oh…she'd tried to hide it from him, and whenever they were in bed together she'd succeeded in convincing him everything between them was almost perfect.

But he'd sensed her growing resentment of the fact he left her alone all day, and he'd recognized the signs of boredom and restlessness.

He just hadn't known what to do. And gradually he'd reached the conclusion he had to let her go, had to set her free to find herself, believing if their love was meant to be, their paths would cross again.

What he hadn't anticipated was the agony of seeing the pain and confusion in her eyes when he set her adrift, or the anguish of knowing he was solely responsible for that pain.

He'd made a mistake, one of the biggest mistakes of his life, and he'd paid dearly for his error in judgment. He'd lost the only woman he'd ever really loved.

When she'd walked out on him he'd respected her need to get away from him. It hadn't been until a few hours later that he'd learned she'd hopped a cab to the airport. That's when he'd hightailed it after her, but by the time he got there he'd heard on the car radio about the crash of the small commuter plane that had killed his friends.

Evan hadn't seen or spoken to Jade since that tragic night over a year ago, and when she'd blown in with the storm in search of his father, she'd thrown him for a loop.

But in the space of one night, not only had she succeeded in winning over the heart of a small boy aching for a mother's love, she'd also revived those emotions he'd safely locked away.

When Kelly had made the comment about him needing a wife, he'd seen it as an answer to his prayers. And while his first priority had been to safeguard Matthew's future, he'd had another reason, a much more personal reason—indeed, a selfish reason—for asking Jade to be his wife. He was damned if he was going to lose her a second time.

But he'd hadn't bargained on Jade laying down some rules of her own. Her announcement that their marriage would be a marriage in name only had, to say the least, stunned him, but he'd readily accepted her terms, silently telling himself time was on his side.

Time to chip away at the wall she'd built around her heart; time to rebuild their relationship on a new and better foundation; time to slowly woo her and win back her heart.

It wouldn't be easy. But something worth fighting for never was. He had to try, if not for his sake, then for Matthew's. Hell! Who was he kidding?

Fate had handed him a second chance. Failure this time was unthinkable.

Chapter Ten

Jade woke with a start. As her gaze darted around the hotel room, the events of the previous night suddenly came rushing back. Not for the first time since she'd walked away from Evan, she felt a stab of regret.

She'd spent a restless night, tossing and turning, trying unsuccessfully to ignore the ache of unfulfilled desire as well as the feeling of emptiness tugging at her heart.

Evan's kiss had reawakened needs she'd thought were buried deep in her heart, and her body had been eager and all too willing to know again the wonder of his possession.

Like a sand castle in the path of the incoming tide, her attempt to keep him at arm's length had collapsed under the onslaught of the very first wave.

Evan had been the one to rein in the desire running rampant through them and remind her of the line she'd drawn between them when she'd insisted their marriage be a marriage in name only.

What if Evan hadn't stopped? She shivered as the need he'd evoked with just one kiss surfaced once more. But while there was no doubt in her mind Evan's lovemaking would have been incredibly exciting and wonderfully satisfying, in the cold light of day she knew she would have regretted her actions, hated herself for not having the strength to resist.

Pushing the bedcovers aside, Jade took a step toward the chair by the bed where she'd tossed the terry-cloth robe before climbing naked into bed.

A knock startled her, and when the door opened she snatched up the robe, holding it against her like a protective shield.

"Jade...oh...I'm sorry." As Evan's gaze slid over her, Jade saw the flare of desire that came and went in his eyes before he turned away.

"Is something wrong? Is Matthew all right?" she asked, ignoring the heat sprinting through her veins as she scrambled into the robe.

"Matthew's fine," Evan responded. He threw a cursory glance over his shoulder. "I called the airline. Medford Airport has been reopened," he went on, turning to face her. "Our flight leaves in an hour."

"Oh...I see. I'll be ready in five minutes," she assured him.

The moment Evan withdrew, Jade hurried into the bathroom to retrieve her underclothes. After dressing in her slacks and sweater, she carefully folded her wedding outfit and placed it in the shopping bag.

Her hands lingered for a moment on the silk jacket and she let out a heartfelt sigh. Last night should have been the first night of her honeymoon...the start of her life with Evan.

But she'd chosen to sleep alone. It was a choice she'd have to live with...a choice she was already beginning to regret.

When the taxi driver pulled up outside the airport they only had a scant ten minutes before the flight was scheduled to leave. Throughout the drive from the hotel Matthew had seemed a little out of sorts, but when Jade asked how he was feeling, he'd smiled and told her he was fine.

Their late arrival at the check-in counter resulted in more seating problems, but there were two seats together and Evan suggested Matthew sit with Jade.

As the plane taxied down the runway, Matthew flashed her a smile and Jade felt somewhat reassured as his blue eyes sparkled with excitement.

During the short flight, Jade asked Matthew questions about his school in Boston and he answered, telling her stories about his friends and teacher.

After they arrived in Medford, Jade helped Matthew with his jacket and backpack and soon they were leaving the terminal and were on their way to the parking lot.

Jade shivered and hugged her jacket about her when she saw the snow piled outside. San Francisco with its sunshine and warmer temperatures seemed nothing more than a distant memory.

Evan said little as he started the engine and headed toward the highway. The roads appeared to be in much the same condition as they had been on their journey south.

An hour later Evan stopped at a roadside café and they ate a bite of lunch. Matthew picked at his food and ate very little, but Jade made no comment.

On the pretext of brushing his hair out of his eyes she let her hand linger a moment on his forehead, trying to gauge whether or not there was any need for concern.

While Matthew seemed slightly warm to her touch, Jade wasn't sure whether it was due to the hot air blasting from a heater in the café or from an elevated temperature.

After lunch they resumed their journey, and when Matthew dozed off, Jade relaxed a little. Evan had hardly spoken a word since leaving the hotel in San Francisco, and a quick glance at his handsome profile only served to heighten the tension thrumming through her.

Half an hour later the silence was shattered by a loud moan from the back seat.

"Oooooh…my tummy hurts!" Matthew wailed. Jade twisted around in her seat to see tears streaming down the boy's face.

"Oh…Matthew, don't cry. Are you going to be sick?" Jade asked, her concern for him mounting by the second.

"No…I don't know…." Matthew responded jerkily between sobs.

Evan glanced over his shoulder at Matthew.

"Hey, sport. We're not far from Paradise," he said in a calm voice. "It's only a couple of miles up the road," he went on. "We'll stop at the hospital and get a doctor to take a look at you. Hang in there, buddy, okay?''

Matthew nodded but kept on moaning.

''Atta boy!'' Evan gave him an encouraging smile.

Evan quickly turned his attention to the road ahead and gently added pressure to the gas pedal. But much as he wanted to put the pedal to the floor, he resisted the temptation.

Fear for Matthew clawed at his insides and he had to force himself to maintain a steady speed, intent on keeping the truck on the road and avoiding the very real possibility of hitting an icy patch and sliding into the nearest snowbank.

Jade's hand on his arm startled him, but even as he darted a questioning glance at her, he found the contact infinitely reassuring, helping to subdue the panic building inside him.

''I'm going to climb into the back seat,'' she said, and before he could respond she unsnapped her seat belt and scrambled over the front seat.

''Oh…my tummy…it really hurts.…'' Matthew groaned as Jade maneuvered herself into the seat beside him.

Putting her arm around his shoulder, she hugged him to her, wishing she didn't feel so helpless. Fifteen heart-wrenching minutes later Evan pulled into the driveway of the hospital on the outskirts of Paradise.

The truck skidded to a halt in front of the hospital's emergency entrance and Evan was out of his seat in a flash. Opening the rear passenger door, he leaned in and, after releasing Matthew's seat belt, scooped the boy into his arms. Jade climbed out and hurried after Evan.

"My boy's sick…he needs a doctor," Evan told the nurse who came to meet them.

"Come right this way," the nurse instructed as she strode past the desk toward a row of curtained cubicles. "Put him on the bed. I'll get a doctor," the nurse said before closing the curtains.

Evan lowered Matthew onto the hospital bed and removed the boy's jacket. Jade met Evan's gaze and, seeing the tortured look in the depths of his eyes, her heart went out to him.

Tears were streaming down Matthew's face and he whimpered softly. Jade reached for his hand and gave it a squeeze. "Everything's going to be all right, Matthew," she said, relieved that her voice sounded strong and calm.

A little of the fear left Matthew's eyes and he tightened his hold on her hand.

"Hello, folks. I'm Dr. Lawrence." The greeting came from the tall bespectacled young man in a white coat who'd joined them. "What seems to be the problem?"

"It's Matthew," Evan quickly jumped in. "He's been complaining of a sore stomach off and on for the past few days. He suddenly got worse this afternoon," he explained, anxiety in his voice.

"He's also been throwing up," Jade added.

"I see," said Dr. Lawrence, his tone friendly. "Let's take a look, shall we? Hello, Matthew." As he drew level with the boy, he tugged his stethoscope from the pocket of his white coat.

The nurse reappeared. "Perhaps you and your

wife could step outside for a moment while Dr. Lawrence examines him," she said, holding the curtains open.

Matthew threw Evan a concerned glance.

"You'll be fine," the doctor assured Matthew. "I promise this won't take long," he added.

Jade lifted Matthew's hand and kissed it.

"We'll be right outside," she said before following Evan from the cubicle.

"There's a waiting area by the desk," the nurse informed them, pointing to an alcove where several chairs were already occupied.

As Evan slowly made his way to the waiting area Jade noted the droop of his shoulders and the worry etched on his handsome features. Wanting to offer comfort, she reached out and caught his hand in hers.

Evan stopped and turned to look at her, a curious expression on his face.

"Matthew's going to be fine," she said softly giving his hand a squeeze.

An emotion she couldn't quite decipher flickered in his eyes, and the air between them crackled with tension.

When Evan's fingers tightened their hold on hers, her breath caught in her throat as something warm and wonderful embraced her.

The moment was over in a flash as Evan's glance slid past her. Releasing her, he moved to meet the man hurrying toward them.

"What is it? What's wrong with Matthew? Is it serious?" Evan asked his tone urgent.

"Your son has acute appendicitis and he needs

surgery immediately,'' Dr. Lawrence replied evenly. ''There's no time to waste.''

''Appendicitis!'' Evan repeated in a shocked voice.

''A classic case…'' the doctor confirmed. ''You'll have to excuse me…Mr.….''

''Mathieson. Evan Mathieson,'' he supplied.

''Mr. Mathieson,'' the doctor acknowledged. ''A nurse will be here with the pertinent forms for you to sign. As soon as the operation is over, I'll be back down to talk to you.'' With that, the doctor spun away, leaving Jade and Evan staring after him in stunned silence.

''My God! Poor kid…'' Evan muttered. ''What if—'' He broke off abruptly and began to pace, raking both hands through his hair in a gesture that spoke volumes.

''Evan…Matthew's in good hands. He's going to be fine,'' Jade said, not sure if she was trying to reassure him or herself.

The hour that followed was one of the worst in Jade's memory. A nurse appeared with forms for Evan to fill out and sign, keeping him occupied at least for a time.

Jade couldn't recall ever seeing Evan so tense or so afraid, and she wished with all her heart there was something she could do or say that would ease his mind.

But in truth she was having problems of her own, constantly fighting down feelings of nausea. Ever since her stay in the hospital in Los Angeles, when she'd lost their baby, she'd developed an aversion to the smell of the antiseptic that permeated the air in most hospitals.

Fearful she might be sick, she rose from the chair next to Evan. "I'll be right back. I'm going to find a bathroom," she muttered before heading down the corridor.

In the washroom Jade splashed cold water on her face and took several deep breaths in the hope of alleviating the nausea plaguing her. But the queasy feeling remained.

When she returned to the waiting area five minutes later there was no sign of Evan. She quickly crossed to the nurses' desk.

"Ah…Mrs. Mathieson, your husband asked me to tell you that your son is out of surgery and he's fine," said the nurse.

Relief flooded through Jade and she blinked away the tears suddenly blurring her vision. "Thank you," she said.

"Your husband is with Dr. Lawrence. He insisted on being taken to the recovery room to see your son," she explained. "They'll be taking Matthew to a room on the fifth floor—that's our pediatric floor. You're welcome to wait for them there. The elevators are just around the corner," she added pleasantly.

"Thank you," Jade said again, but instead of heading to the elevators, she crossed to the waiting area and, snatching her sheepskin jacket from the chair, made a beeline for the doors leading outside.

Jade swallowed several mouthfuls of the crisp fresh air as she pulled on her coat. Late afternoon shadows made the view somewhat gloomy, but she stood for several minutes in the brisk icy wind, enjoying the feel of it tugging at her hair. Feeling marginally better, she made her way back through the automatic doors.

"Jade! There you are," Evan said as he came to meet her. "Did the nurse tell you? Matthew's fine. I just saw him." The relief in his voice was palpable.

"Yes, she told me. That's wonderful," Jade responded. "Was he awake?" she asked as she shrugged out of her jacket.

Evan shook his head. "I don't think he even knew I was there," he said with a rueful smile.

"Can we go and see him now?" she asked.

"I came back down to get you," Evan went on. "They've moved him to the pediatric floor. Dr. Lawrence said we can peek in on him, but just for a few minutes."

"What are we waiting for?" Jade replied.

"Hey, Matthew. How's it going? Feeling better?" Jade asked softly as she approached the pale figure on the bed. He looked so small, so vulnerable, Jade felt tears prick her eyes when she bent to kiss his cheek.

Matthew managed a weak smile. "Hi," he said with a tired sigh. "I had an operation," he added as his gaze shifted to where Evan stood on the opposite side of the bed.

"We know," Evan said with a low chuckle as he brushed a lock of Matthew's hair from his forehead.

Matthew licked his lips before continuing. "I'll

have to stay here, won't I?'' he asked, anxiety evident in his voice.

''I don't think you're in any shape to leave, just yet, sport. Do you?'' Evan replied easily.

''No…''

''Just think what you'll have to tell your friends when you get back to Boston,'' Jade said, hoping to shift Matthew's thoughts in another direction.

The anxious look in Matthew's eyes faded a little, replaced by the faint glimmer of excitement. ''Yeah…and I can show everybody my staples.…'' he said with a sleepy grin.

Evan's low rumble of laughter rippled over Jade like a warm breeze.

''Staples! That's gruesome stuff,'' Evan said. ''I bet the kids will all be jealous,'' he teased.

''So…how's my patient?'' asked Dr. Lawrence as he joined them. ''Feeling better?'' He picked up the chart from the foot of the bed and quickly scanned it.

''A little,'' Matthew said.

''Well, young fella, we removed your appendix and now you won't be getting any more of those nasty tummy aches. Unless of course you eat too much cake and ice cream.'' He smiled.

''When can I go home?'' Matthew asked.

''In a few days. You're a healthy young fella and you'll recover quickly,'' Dr. Lawrence assured him. ''But right now you need to get some sleep. When you wake up in the morning you'll be feeling a whole lot better.''

''Okay,'' Matthew said on a sigh, obviously too

tired to protest, his eyelids already beginning to drift shut.

Evan squeezed Matthew's hand, then leaned over and dropped a light kiss on his forehead.

"Jade and I will be back first thing in the morning," Evan said, but Matthew's eyes were already closed and he made no reply.

"The nurses will keep an eye on him, but I don't anticipate any problems," said Dr. Lawrence as they quietly left the room. "He's one lucky kid," the doctor went on. "His appendix could have ruptured at any time and that would have complicated matters considerably. But we got to him in time and he'll be as good as new in a few days."

"That's wonderful. Thank you," Jade managed to respond, refusing to even think about what might have happened if they hadn't brought Matthew to the hospital in time.

"Perhaps you could let the nurse on the floor know where you can be reached," the doctor continued. "I'll check in on Matthew again in the morning."

"We'll do that. Thank you, Dr. Lawrence." Evan shook the doctor's hand. With a smile and a polite nod to Jade, the doctor moved off down the corridor.

"It's too far to drive to the cabin," Evan said as they walked toward the nurses' desk. "We could stay at the Lodge on Main Street," he suggested.

"Fine," Jade replied.

Evan related this information to the nurse at the desk while Jade waited by the elevators. Her nausea was slowly intensifying, and when the elevator doors opened she practically fell inside. Evan joined her and she quickly pressed the button for the main floor.

"Jade, what's wrong? You've gone as white as a sheet," Evan said, his hands coming up to grip her shoulders.

A jolt of heat sprinted through her at his touch, and she swallowed convulsively before lifting her gaze to meet his. "I don't like hospitals. The smell makes me nauseous," she told him, and felt tears sting her eyes when he gently pulled her into his arms.

"Why didn't you say something?" Evan scolded softly, his hand stroking her back, effectively distracting her and making her forget the wild tilting of her stomach. "You never told me...." he accused.

Jade leaned into him. It felt so good to have his arms around her, to feel his strength. She sighed. "It only started happening recently, ever since—" She stopped abruptly, biting down on her lip to cut off her confession.

"Ever since what?" Evan asked as the elevator slowed to a halt.

"Nothing... It doesn't matter," she mumbled, relieved when the doors slid open on the main floor, where several people stood waiting. "Please, I just need some fresh air," she said, though she had to admit being in Evan's arms made her forget everything.

The chilly early-evening air helped soothe Jade's frayed nerves, and when she climbed into the passenger seat of the four by four, she managed a weak smile.

The Lodge on Main Street was an old three-storied hotel that, according to a sign taped to the front door, had recently undergone renovations.

Evan approached the reception desk and rang the bell sitting atop the gleaming oak counter.

"Hello!" A voice greeted them and they turned to see a short attractive woman in her late fifties striding toward them, wiping her hands on a dish towel.

"Hi…we'd like a couple of rooms, please," Evan began.

"You're Hank Mathieson's son, aren't you?" the woman said, ignoring his request.

Evan frowned. "Yes—"

"I thought so. You look just like your father," their host continued. "He talks about you a lot. You're the reporter on the television, aren't you?" she asked, but before Evan could answer she hurried on. "How is Hank? Haven't seen him in town for a while. Heading up to see him, are you?"

"Yes…ah, Hank's fine," Evan responded, feeling a little dizzy from the barrage of questions.

"Glad to hear it. By the way, I'm Mildred Wilson, Millie to my friends," the woman introduced herself. "We've known your father ever since my hubby and I bought the Lodge…my, it must be nearly eight years ago," she went on as she slung the towel over her left shoulder.

"Really…" Evan said, throwing Jade a look of appeal.

"I'm sorry…did you say you and your wife wanted a room?" Millie asked, slipping behind the oak counter.

Evan hesitated for a moment before answering. ''That's right,'' he replied, casting Jade an apologetic glance.

''Well...you can have your pick of the place tonight,'' she went on cheerily. ''Not many folks on the road at this time of year and especially not in this kind of weather,'' she added as she retrieved a leather-bound book from beneath the counter. ''Room eight is very nice,'' she said after a quick consultation.

''Thank you,'' Evan said.

''Oh...and would you be having dinner?'' Millie asked as she spun the book around and handed Evan a pen. ''Our cook does us proud. He lives just down the street, thank goodness, otherwise all I could offer you tonight would be beans on toast.'' She laughed. ''But I'll have you know folks come from far and wide to eat here, and it's no wonder, 'cause the food is pretty darned good, if I do say so myself.''

Evan glanced at Jade as he scribbled his signature on the line below Millie's index finger and Jade saw the twinkle of humor in his eyes.

''Thank you. Dinner would be lovely,'' Jade said, feeling her mouth twitch in response.

''Would you like to eat now?'' she asked. ''Or would you like to check out your room first?''

''Let's eat now, shall we?'' Evan suggested.

''Fine...'' Jade replied, relieved at the thought of postponing their trip upstairs. This time they'd be sharing a room, and that thought alone sent a shiver of awareness chasing down her spine. But Millie Wilson hadn't really given Evan much choice in the matter.

"Good…" Millie readily approved their decision. "Let me give you a key to your room," she went on. "It's on the first floor. That's up the stairs, down the hall and the first door on your right." She handed Evan the key. "Now then, if you'll follow me, the dining room is right this way."

Millie Wilson came from behind the counter and headed in the direction from which she'd first appeared.

Evan helped Jade off with her jacket as they followed their host. The room was large and spacious and beautifully decorated in shades of purple and pink that reminded Jade of the colors of a sunset.

Millie led them toward a table for two near the enormous fireplace, where real logs burned in the grate and a glowing warmth radiated into the room adding a wonderful ambiance to the place.

"What a beautiful room…." Jade said as she lowered herself into the captain's chair.

"Thank you," Millie said. "Frank, that's my husband, he picked the colors. Don't they look great? Mind you, I'm color-blind myself, but everyone who comes in here says he's done a fabulous job—"

"Indeed he has," Evan cut in, flashing his hostess a smile.

"Here's the menu… I'll get Jill to take your order. She's my granddaughter," Millie explained. "She's saving up for college. I never went to college myself, but that's neither here nor there—"

"Thank you, Millie," Evan interrupted, hoping she would take the hint.

"I'll leave you to it," she responded, taking no

offense. "Enjoy your meal," she added before hurrying away.

"Phew! I'm worn out," Evan said as he opened the menu.

Jade laughed softly. "She had that effect on me, too," she replied.

"I'm sorry about only getting one room," Evan said. "But it just seemed simpler...."

"I agree...." Jade said, annoyed to feel her face growing warm.

"We'll figure something out. In the meantime let's just enjoy dinner," Evan suggested before turning to the menu.

The sound of soft laughter coming from somewhere nearby drew Jade's attention, and she glanced across the room to see a couple sitting at a table tucked into the alcove on the other side of the fireplace.

Jade couldn't help noticing that the woman was pregnant, very pregnant, and for a brief moment she felt her heart shudder to a halt at the look of pure joy and happiness on the other woman's face as she gazed at the man with her.

Tears stung Jade's eyes and she quickly dropped her gaze as feelings of sadness and regret suddenly overwhelmed her.

It was with some relief she heard their young waitress approach. Blinking back the moisture gathering in her eyes, Jade tried to focus on the menu.

Unlike her talkative grandmother, Jill kept her words to a minimum, and after taking their order smiled shyly before retreating to the kitchen.

The cosy atmosphere generated by the flames

flickering in the fireplace and the muted lighting from the candles on the tables and sundry lighting somehow set the tone. And once again, conversation, centered mostly on Matthew, flowed easily.

There were times throughout the meal Jade found her gaze straying to the couple in the alcove, catching a glimpse of the tender smiles they exchanged, the lingering touches, and hearing their shared laughter.

A feeling of envy tugged sharply at Jade, and not for the first time she found herself wishing she could turn the clock back…return to those days during their engagement when she'd believed nothing could ever come between her and Evan.

But she'd been wrong! Evan hadn't been happy. Why else would he have broken their engagement? And if she was totally honest with herself…she hadn't been happy, either.

The realization stunned her, but she knew in her heart it was true. And with an insight she wished she'd had a year ago, she recognized she had only herself to blame.

No wonder Evan had grown tired of her. She'd behaved like an adolescent fool, believing naively that in order to sustain the fires burning between them she had to spend every waking moment with him.

That's why she'd insisted on dropping out of college to accompany him on his assignments…and because she'd had nothing to focus her mind on, she'd grown bored and restless with each passing day and, like a child deprived of a parent's attention, ever resentful of the time he'd spent away from her.

She saw now, with a clarity that almost made her squirm, how incredibly immature she'd been to think any relationship could survive in those conditions.

But she'd grown up a lot during the past year. She'd had to. Having gone through the highly traumatic and emotionally draining ordeal of losing their baby, she'd learned a lot about herself—and more than she'd ever wanted to know about the pain and heartache of loving and losing.

Completing her degree and finding a job had helped instill a greater sense of self-confidence, a confidence she'd lacked back then.

Fool! She silently chastised herself, realizing for the very first time just how much she had truly lost.

"Jade?" Evan said gently.

"Sorry…" Jade responded and, careful to avoid his gaze, she folded her napkin and placed it on the table.

"Here's the key," Evan said. "I thought you might like to head upstairs first. I'll give the hospital one quick call and then join you," he said evenly.

"Thank you," Jade replied, touched by the fact he was affording her the opportunity to go upstairs alone. That he was obviously abiding by the rules she'd set forth was commendable, but as she wound her way from the dining room Jade found herself wishing she had the courage to tell Evan she'd changed her mind about wanting a marriage of convenience, that she loved him with all her heart—that she wanted their marriage to be real.

Chapter Eleven

The door to room eight was unlocked and Evan quietly let himself in, noting with a mixed sense of relief and disappointment that there were two beds.

Jade had chosen the bed beneath the window, and he stood for a moment listening to the sound of her deep breathing before inching closer to gaze down at the woman who was now his wife.

Her autumn gold hair was spread across the pillow like a splash of paint and he allowed himself the luxury of studying her almost-classic features, features that were already etched in his memory.

Her heart-shaped face was stunning in repose, and the urge to lay a trail of kisses across her forehead, over her high cheekbones to her pert little nose and down to her lips, was overwhelming.

Evan drew a tortured breath feeling his body grow tense with the need he'd evoked. An avalanche of emotions bombarded him, emotions he struggled to control. And not for the first time he wondered at his wisdom in agreeing to a marriage that wasn't a marriage at all.

But he'd been desperate to do what was necessary for Matthew—and desperate to keep Jade in his life. And while he wasn't proud of the fact he'd deliberately manipulated her and knew, too, his actions had been both arrogant and reckless, he was honest enough to admit that if push came to shove, he'd do it again in a minute.

Wearily he sat down on the edge of the empty bed and dropped his head in his hands. His thoughts turned to the dramatic events of the afternoon, remembering with clarity the fear and panic he'd barely been able to control.

Jade's very presence, her quiet confidence and calm demeanor throughout the ordeal, had prevented a very frightened Matthew from becoming hysterical and had gone a long way to take the edge off his own fear.

He wasn't sure he would have made it through the anxious wait for the doctor to return if she hadn't been there with him. The mere thought of life without her conjured up a bleak and unhappy future for both him and Matthew.

He admired the fact that she'd rallied after their breakup and gone on to finish her degree and forge a career for herself. Her self-confidence had grown and there was a new maturity in her eyes, along with a sadness that tugged at his heart.

He glanced at Jade's sleeping figure. The temptation to pull back the covers and climb in beside her was almost more than he could resist.

He recalled vividly the times during their four months together when he had returned to the hotel in the early hours of the morning to slip naked beneath the covers, and gently pull her warm, unresisting body against his.

He had kissed her soft mouth until her lips parted to allow his tongue access to tease and taste. Her sleepy sighs of pleasure had swiftly changed to whimpers of need, and she had eagerly returned his kisses, until they'd both been wide-awake and trembling with desire.

Evan stood up abruptly and headed for the bathroom, cursing under his breath at letting his memories run riot. Locking the door, he stripped and turned on the shower.

The icy spray made him gasp, but he gritted his teeth and reminded himself that he'd agreed to Jade's request for a marriage of convenience. He prided himself in being a man who kept his promises, whatever the cost.

When Jade awakened the next morning, she quickly scanned the bedroom, relieved to discover she was alone. Though the rumpled bed next to her indicated Evan had indeed slept there, he'd obviously risen early and gone downstairs.

Glancing at the clock on the bedside table she saw it was just seven-thirty and, pushing the covers aside, she grabbed her slacks and sweater and headed for the bathroom.

A hot shower washed away the remnants of sleep, and after toweling herself she dried her hair with the hair dryer hanging on the bathroom wall.

When she emerged from the bathroom her heart faltered for a moment at the sight of Evan in his shirtsleeves and gray slacks, sitting at the small table near the window.

"Good morning," Evan greeted her, and as he met her gaze a smile curved invitingly at the corners of his mouth, a smile that sent her pulses racing.

"Hi!" she said, feeling strangely shy.

"Are you hungry? Shall we grab breakfast or would you rather just head to the hospital?" Evan asked.

"Won't Matthew be waiting for us?" Jade responded as she moved to the alcove to retrieve her jacket, thinking they could pick up something on the way to the hospital.

"Most likely," Evan said. "But I thought it might be easier for you…at the hospital, that is, if you've eaten first."

A warm feeling enfolded her when she realized his concern was for her, silently acknowledging that eating first would slow down the onslaught of her nausea, but she was anxious to see Matthew and felt sure Evan shared her feelings.

"I'll be fine," she said. "Let's go and see how Matthew's doing." She turned to find Evan standing beside her, and for the second time in as many minutes her heart jolted against her rib cage and a familiar heat surged through her veins.

"There's a cafeteria at the hospital. We can pick up something there," he said easily. "Oh…by the way…I want you to know how much I appreciate all you did yesterday."

Jade felt the color rise in her cheeks at the warmth

she could hear in his voice. "I didn't do anything," she responded.

"Feeling the way you do about hospitals, I'd argue that point," he countered with a smile.

Jade was silent as they made their way down to the main floor. Outside, the sun was shining and though the air was decidedly chilly, the cloudless blue sky promised a brighter day.

At the hospital Evan had no trouble finding an empty space in the parking lot. Jade grabbed Matthew's backpack from the rear seat, thinking he might be feeling up to playing a game of checkers.

Matthew's face lit up when they entered his room. "Hi! I thought you guys were never gonna get here," he said.

"Hi, yourself!" Jade responded as she bent to kiss Matthew's cheek, relieved to see he looked more like his old self and silently marveling at the recuperative powers of young children. "How are you feeling this morning?"

"Better," came the quick reply. "The staples feel a bit funny and they hurt if I move too much," he told her. "Oh…great! You brought my backpack," he exclaimed happily when she dropped it on the bed beside him.

"Jade figured you might be up to playing a game of checkers," Evan said as he gently ruffled Matthew's hair and squeezed his shoulder. "I see you have a roommate today," Evan went on, referring to the young boy in the other bed.

Matthew nodded. "That's Blair—he fell off the top bunk at his friend's house in the middle of the night and broke his arm," he explained.

"Ouch...I bet that hurt." Evan threw Blair a sympathetic smile.

"Has Dr. Lawrence been in to see you yet?" Jade asked.

"Yeah," Matthew replied.

"What did he say?" Evan asked.

"Nothing much...but he wants me to stay in the hospital for a few more days," Matthew reported.

"How do you feel about that?" Evan asked.

"It's okay, I guess...." Matthew said. "The nurses are nice and they said I can get up later and take a walk to the playroom down the hall. They've got a TV there and books and games and stuff," he told them.

"Sounds cool," Evan commented.

"I guess you've already had breakfast," Jade said.

"Yeah, I had some fruit and a glass of milk," Matthew said.

"I could use a cup of coffee. How about you?" Jade asked Evan. She was already beginning to feel nauseous and thought a quick trip outside in the fresh air would do the trick.

"Sounds good," Evan responded, and for a fleeting moment he held her gaze, silently communicating that he knew the real reason for her departure.

"Why don't you set up the board for checkers and I'll play the winner when I come back," she suggested.

"Okay!" Matthew eagerly agreed.

Jade withdrew and headed toward the fifth-floor nurses' desk and the elevators. She punched the elevator button, but after waiting several minutes decided she'd be quicker using the stairs.

Glancing around, she spotted the Exit sign at the far end of the corridor and hurried toward it.

All at once the atmosphere of the hospital floor changed and Jade heard the sound of a baby crying and smelled the sweet scent of baby powder.

With a start she realized she'd ventured into the maternity section. Her footsteps slowed to a halt as she drew level with the window overlooking the nursery. Jade stopped and let her gaze roam over the row of tiny bassinets.

Her breath locked in her throat at the sight of four tiny babies wrapped snugly in their blankets. She scanned the faces of the newborn infants, feeling as if her heart was being squeezed in a vise. Tears gathered in her eyes and her lungs ached with the effort not to cry.

Her nausea forgotten, she rested her forehead on the cool glass and an errant teardrop spilled down her cheek for the child she'd loved and lost.

"Excuse me. Are you all right?"

Jade drew a startled breath and, brushing away the moisture with the back of her hand, turned to the person who'd spoken.

Recognition was instantaneous as Jade found herself face-to-face with the pregnant young woman who, along with her husband, had been the only other occupants of the restaurant last night.

"Oh…it's you!" Jade exclaimed, noticing the woman was wearing a hospital gown.

The young woman frowned. "Do I know you?" she asked.

"I'm sorry," Jade muttered with embarrassment. "No, you don't know me," she confessed. "It's just that—I saw you last night—"

Recognition flashed in the other woman's eyes. "Of course," she interrupted. "I remember now. You and your husband were eating dinner in the Lodge dining room."

"Yes…" Jade replied. "Did you have your baby?" she asked, glancing at her hospital gown.

The woman laughed. "Yes…I went into labor right after we left the restaurant," she explained.

"Wow!" Jade responded. "Everything must have gone well. What did you have?"

"A beautiful, healthy baby girl," the woman replied, her voice echoing with both love and pride. "We're calling her Nicole."

"How wonderful! Congratulations!" Jade said sincerely.

The woman's smile was radiant. "Thank you," she responded. "By the way, I'm Lauren Stornoway."

"Jade Ad—Jade Mathieson," she said, tripping over her new name.

"Nicole is right there in the first bassinet," Lauren continued, moving closer to the viewing window.

Jade followed the woman's gaze to the baby wrapped in a pink blanket, her tiny face serene in sleep, a peachlike fuzz of dark hair on her head.

"She's so beautiful," Jade admired, her voice husky.

"Mark says she looks like an angel," Lauren boasted with a smile. "Mark—he's my husband," she explained unnecessarily, "—is simply over the moon. He was so worried because I had two miscarriages before this pregnancy, and as you can imagine we were both concerned. But everything went amazingly well and now we have a lovely daughter...."

Jade felt tears sting her eyes once more.

"I'm sorry. Have I said something to upset you?" Lauren put her hand on Jade's arm.

"No...really, I'm fine," Jade said. "It's just that I—" She broke off, surprised she'd almost confided her loss to this woman who was a stranger.

"Please, I'd like to help," Lauren said kindly.

Jade drew a steadying breath. "I had a miscarriage about a year ago," she said, and at her words saw the look of compassion and understanding that came into the other woman's eyes.

"I'm so sorry," Lauren said.

"It's silly, I know, but just looking at babies..." Jade stopped and swallowed the hard ball of emotion clogging her throat.

"No, it's not silly. I do understand...believe me," Lauren said. "But you and your husband shouldn't give up hope." She reached out and closed her hand over Jade's.

Pain seared Jade's heart, momentarily clouding her vision.

"Thank you," Jade mumbled. "Excuse me...I'm sorry, I have to go," she added before moving past the new mother and out through the exit door a few feet beyond.

Jade ran down the flight of stairs as if a mad dog

were chasing her. When she burst into the parking lot, tears were streaming down her face.

She leaned against the door, panting for breath as Lauren Stornoway's words of comfort and encouragement echoed inside her head. But Jade's tears weren't only for the loss of her child.

Not for the first time Jade wished she'd been strong enough to resist Evan's plea for help, wished she hadn't insisted on a marriage of convenience, wished she wasn't deeply and irrevocably in love with a man who didn't love her.

"Evan, you're not watching," Matthew scolded as he picked up a black game piece and jumped Evan's remaining red ones before removing them all from the board.

"Oh...darn it all, you're right," Evan said ruefully as he slid off the bed. His thoughts were on Jade. She'd been gone more than half an hour and his concern for her was growing.

All at once the door to Matthew's room swung open and Evan turned with some relief to see Jade enter carrying two steaming cups of coffee.

"Jade, there you are! I was beginning to think you'd gotten lost," Evan said, giving her a frowning glance as she advanced toward him.

"I've beat Evan three times already," Matthew told her happily. "Now it's your turn to play."

"Sorry," Jade said. "There was a lineup in the cafeteria."

"Thanks." Evan accepted the coffee Jade held out to him, noticing as he did how she deliberately avoided meeting his gaze.

"All right! Set up the board," Jade ordered with forced cheerfulness. "Hey! Where's your room-mate?" she asked as she dropped her jacket on the chair next to the bed.

"Blair's mom and dad came and took him home," Matthew replied as he began to arrange the game pieces on the board.

Evan stood on the sidelines sipping coffee. Over the rim of the paper cup he studied Jade and noticed the redness in her eyes, a sure sign she'd been cry-ing.

Anger and a fierce sense of protectiveness surged through him, but much as he wanted to ask what was wrong, who had made her cry, now was neither the time nor the place.

A moment later a nurse entered to check on Mat-thew. After taking his temperature and peeking at his dressing, she withdrew and the checker game began, but Jade found her concentration wavering, aware in no small way of Evan staring at her.

"Rats and mice," Matthew said a few minutes later after completing a move.

"Where?" Jade responded, spinning around in search of the rodents. Her reaction sent Matthew into a fit of laughter, which quickly changed to moans.

"Oh…please…don't make me laugh," he pleaded. "It hurts.…" He clutched his abdomen with both hands. "I moved the wrong one," he said, nodding at the board.

"Oh…!" Jade glanced at the game board and saw Matthew had made a horrendous move. Flashing a wicked grin, Jade picked up one of her game pieces and cleared the remainder of Matthew's from the board. "I won! I actually won! With some help from the rats and mice," she added cheekily.

Matthew broke into renewed laughter, accompanied by fresh moans.

The sound of Evan's deep rumble of laughter coming from directly behind her had Jade spinning around, and when their glances collided, she felt a quiver of longing race through her.

"The winner and new champion," Evan said, and grasping Jade's wrist, raised her hand high, like a referee at a prize fight.

"Oooh…no fair…" Matthew groaned, but he was grinning from ear to ear, his eyes sparkling with good humor.

Evan brought Jade's arm down to her side but he held on to her wrist, feeling the delicate bones beneath his fingers. Those moments of shared laughter had struck a chord deep inside him, sharply bringing home the feeling that this was what being a family was all about.

For a breathtaking moment their gazes locked, but behind Jade's smile Evan could see a look of abject sorrow that tore at his heart.

"What's all the noise about?" The amused question came from the nurse who'd reentered the room.

Jade wriggled free of Evan's hold and quickly moved away from him.

"Mr. Mathieson?" the nurse said.

"Yes," Evan replied.

"There's a call for you at the nurses' desk," she said.

"Oh…thank you," Evan said, thinking the caller

must be his father. He'd telephoned Hank from the
hotel lobby earlier that morning, briefly explaining
all that had happened and telling him Matthew was
in the hospital in Paradise.

His father's reaction to the news about his marriage to Jade had been one of disbelief, but beneath
the shock Evan was convinced Hank was pleased.

"I'll be right back," Evan said before heading
from the room.

"Would you read me a story?" Matthew asked
once Evan had gone.

"Did you bring *The Wizard of Oz?*" Jade asked.

Matthew nodded. "It's in my backpack," he said
with a tired sigh as he relaxed against the pillows.

Jade cleared away the checkers game, then ex-
tracted the book from Matthew's bag. Pulling up a
chair, she sat down and started to read, but she'd
read only one page when she saw Matthew's eyes
had already drifted shut.

When she heard the door open behind her, she
glanced around and brought a finger to her lips.
"He's asleep," she told the nurse.

"Good. I was coming to suggest you let him rest
for a while. Why don't you come back after lunch,"
said the nurse.

"Good idea," Jade said. Closing the book, she
set it on the bedside table and, retrieving her jacket,
quietly slipped from the room. The smell of antiseptic was stronger in the hallway and Jade felt her
stomach pitch like a boat in a storm.

She threw a quick glance at the nurses' desk, but
when she saw no sign of Evan she ducked into the
nearest washroom and splashed cold water on her

face. Feeling marginally better, she exited the washroom and almost collided with Evan.

"I've been looking for you," he said, an edge to his voice that both startled and puzzled Jade.

"Why?" she asked, noticing the taut line of his jaw and the glitter of anger in his blue eyes.

"We need to talk," Evan responded. "Let's get out of here."

"Evan, what is it? What's wrong?" Jade asked as he ushered her toward the elevators.

"I have some questions that need answers," he said coolly.

Before she could say more, the elevator doors slid open to reveal several occupants. With his hand at her waist, Evan urged her inside, but he remained silent throughout their descent to the main floor, his face a mask she couldn't read.

"The cafeteria's this way," Jade said once they emerged from the elevator. But Evan, his hand still at her back, directed her toward the automatic doors.

"I'm not hungry," he replied. "We have some things that need to be cleared up and I'd much prefer the privacy of a hotel room to the noise and clutter of a cafeteria."

Jade made no response. One glance at Evan told her there was no point arguing, but she was still at a loss to understand his anger.

The drive back to the Lodge was completed in silence. Evan unlocked the door to their room and, tossing his jacket on the newly made bed, began to pace.

Jade removed her jacket and, dropping it on the bed next to Evan's, held her breath and waited.

"Why didn't you tell me?" Evan suddenly broke the tense silence, startling her with the question.

"Tell you what?" Jade asked with a frown, unable to fathom what he was referring to, though there was something in his eyes, something in the way he looked at her, that set off alarm bells.

"That you had a miscarriage," he continued, and watched her green eyes widen with shock and pain.

"How did—" She broke off abruptly and dropped her gaze.

"It *is* true. The woman wasn't lying. My God, Jade…why didn't you tell me you were pregnant?" Evan turned on his heel and began to massage the back of his neck to ease the tension throbbing in his muscles.

"What woman?" Jade asked, but the moment the words were out she realized he had to be talking about Lauren Stornoway.

"The woman from the dining room last night," he explained needlessly, turning to face her once more. "I was standing at the nurses' desk when she walked right up to me. It took me a minute to remember where I knew her from, and by that time she'd told me she'd had her baby and that she'd been talking to my wife earlier.

"Then she started saying how sorry she was about my wife's miscarriage a year ago…that we shouldn't give up hope of having a baby." He stopped and drew a ragged breath.

"I had no idea what she was talking about…then suddenly everything fell into place. No wonder I couldn't track you down… No wonder you didn't show up for Philip and Nina's funeral…. Jade! Why didn't you let me know?'' He held her gaze, his eyes boring into hers, an expression of sadness in their glittering depths.

''Why didn't you tell me you were pregnant, Jade?'' His voice was little more than a throaty whisper now. ''I had a right to know.''

Jade heard the raw emotion in Evan's voice and flinched inwardly at the hurt she could see in his eyes.

''I didn't know....'' she told him, suddenly fighting to hold back the tears welling up inside her. A look of disbelief flashed across Evan's features, and seeing it made a pain twist inside her.

She tried again. ''I had no idea I was pregnant until the doctor at the hospital in L.A. explained the reason for the pains I was having. He told me I might still save the baby if I stayed in the hospital. For three days I just lay there, barely moving, praying for our baby. But...in the end, there was nothing I could do....'' Jade's voice faded as her throat closed over with emotion.

When Evan's hands came up to clasp her shoulders, the temptation to sag against him was almost more than she could resist.

''You lost the baby when you were in L.A.?'' he asked.

''I started having cramps on the plane....'' she explained, and felt him tighten his hold on her. ''They called ahead and an ambulance was waiting at the airport to take me to the hospital.''

''Dear God! Jade!'' All at once he dropped his hands and spun away. ''It was my fault,'' he declared. ''If I hadn't broken our engagement you wouldn't have run off and none of it would have happened—''

''Evan…that's not true,'' Jade was quick to argue. ''It wasn't your fault, it wasn't my fault, it just happened.'' She took a step toward him, wanting to somehow ease his pain, but before she could say more, he spun around to face her.

''It was my fault. Damn it! You went through all that pain…because of me!''

''Evan, don't…'' Jade pleaded.

But he wasn't listening. ''You were so unhappy,'' he hurried on. ''I couldn't bear watching you start to hate me.''

''Hate you?'' Jade repeated incredulously, her voice little more than a harsh whisper.

''Breaking our engagement—letting you go—was the hardest thing I've ever had to do,'' Evan went on, obviously not hearing her. ''After you ran out that night, I went a little crazy. I hadn't meant what I'd said, not one stupid word of it,'' he confessed, and at his words the ache that had been inside Jade's heart for too long began to evaporate like morning mist on the lake.

''I kept telling myself you needed time to make your own way in life…that marriage could wait… but I was wrong to arbitrarily make that decision for you.'' He raked a hand through his hair. ''The doorman at the hotel told me you'd taken a cab to the airport, and that's when I realized I had to try to stop you. But then everything was forgotten when I heard about the plane crash that killed Phil and Nina.''

Jade's heart shuddered to a halt before kicking

into high gear. "Are you saying you were coming to the airport to stop me?" she dared to ask, knowing her future happiness depended on his answer.

Evan met her gaze. "Yes," he said, his tone steeped in self-reproach. "I was a fool to ever let you go."

"Oh...Evan...we both made mistakes," Jade said with fresh insight. "You were right. I wasn't happy," she acknowledged. "But it was with *myself*, not with you," she explained.

"I was insecure about our relationship," she went on. "It all happened so fast. You were a man with vast experience, a man of the world, and though I tried hard, I really wasn't all that self-assured.

"I was afraid once you went back to your job you'd forget about me, meet someone prettier, someone closer to your age, someone—oh...I don't know." She floundered to a halt, realizing how immature and foolish her thinking had been back then.

"I thought if I was with you all the time, I could make you happy...but instead, things between us began to fall apart and I had no idea what to do," she ended on a sigh.

"And I wasn't much help," Evan countered. "I knew something was bothering you, and what I should have done was ask you what was wrong, talk to you about it. Then we could have found a solution together. Instead, I made assumptions and decided to do what I thought was best.

"I was wrong. I made a terrible mistake. A mistake I want to rectify," Evan said in a voice that caused Jade to catch her breath in anticipation.

"How?" Jade asked in a bewildered tone.

Evan swiftly closed the gap between them, and with infinite tenderness captured her face in his hands. "By making this marriage a real marriage, by being the family Matthew wants.... Who am I trying to kid? By becoming the family *I* want us to be, need us to be. Jade, if you'll just let me, I'll make it up to you. I'll never knowingly hurt you again, I promise."

Jade couldn't think, couldn't breathe. Was Evan really saying what she thought he was saying? Before she could even form an answer, Evan touched his mouth to hers in a kiss of such aching tenderness, such exquisite sweetness, she felt her legs buckle under her.

She stumbled against him, her hands coming to rest on his chest. Beneath her fingers she could feel the urgent beat of his heart drumming out a rhythm that almost matched her own.

When he lifted his mouth from hers, she had to bite back the moan of longing hovering on her lips. She drew a quivering breath and opened her eyes to meet his.

"Jade, when I sent you away, I believed I was doing the right thing." His voice was filled with self-reproach. "I was a fool. I can't—won't—lose you again," he vowed, his thumb slowly caressing her lower lip, sending a quicksilver shiver of longing through her.

"Life without you isn't worth living," he went on. "I know you agreed to marry me for Matthew's sake, but I need to know if there's any hope for us.

"I love you. I've never stopped loving you. Is it too much to ask you to forgive me for the pain I've caused? Is it too much to hope that you could love me again?''

Jade felt her heart shudder to a halt in response to Evan's declaration of love. Tears gathered in her eyes.

''Oh…Evan…'' Her heart overflowed with love for him, and at the look of total vulnerability that flashed in his eyes, what little remained of her doubts vanished.

''You don't have to give me an answer now….'' he assured her quickly.

''Yes, I do,'' she contradicted, and felt his body grow tense. ''Evan, I love you. I've never stopped loving you. I'm destined to be yours forever.''

Joy the likes of which he'd never known before exploded inside him, and with a moan of relief he gathered her into his arms and claimed her mouth in a kiss that left no room for doubt in either of their minds.

Several long minutes passed before Evan could bear to break the kiss.

''Did you really say you were mine forever, my darling?'' He smiled into her eyes, knowing he was the luckiest man alive.

''Forever yours,'' she said on a heady sigh.

Evan brought her left hand to his mouth and kissed the gold band he'd placed there only a few days ago.

''My father gave my mother this ring on their wedding day,'' he said. ''He told me he discovered paradise the day he fell in love with her. I know exactly what he meant,'' he said huskily before his

mouth came down to capture hers once more in a
kiss that swept them swiftly on the road to a paradise
of their own.

*   *   *   *   *

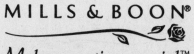

MILLS & BOON®

Makes any time special™

Mills & Boon publish 29 new titles every month. Select from...

Modern Romance™   **Tender Romance**™

Sensual Romance™

Medical Romance™ **Historical Romance**™

MAT2

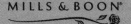

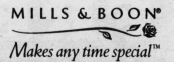

4 FREE

books and a surprise gift!

We would like to take this opportunity to thank you for reading this Mills & Boon® book by offering you the chance to take FOUR more specially selected titles from the Modern Romance™ series absolutely FREE! We're also making this offer to introduce you to the benefits of the Reader Service™—

- ★ FREE home delivery
- ★ FREE gifts and competitions
- ★ FREE monthly Newsletter
- ★ Exclusive Reader Service discounts
- ★ Books available before they're in the shops

Accepting these FREE books and gift places you under no obligation to buy, you may cancel at any time, even after receiving your free shipment. Simply complete your details below and return the entire page to the address below. *You don't even need a stamp!*

YES! Please send me 4 free Modern Romance books and a surprise gift. I understand that unless you hear from me, I will receive 6 superb new titles every month for just £2.40 each, postage and packing free. I am under no obligation to purchase any books and may cancel my subscription at any time. The free books and gift will be mine to keep in any case.

P0ZEA

Ms/Mrs/Miss/Mr ....Initials....................................
BLOCK CAPITALS PLEASE

Surname ....

Address ....

....

....Postcode....................................

Send this whole page to:
UK: FREEPOST CN81, Croydon, CR9 3WZ
EIRE: PO Box 4546, Kilcock, County Kildare (stamp required)

Together for the first time
3 compelling novels by
bestselling author

PENNY
JORDAN

The
Bride's
BOUQUET

One wedding — one bouquet —
leads to three trips to the altar

Published on 22nd September

MILLS & BOON®

0010/116/MB6